URBAN SHOTS
YUVA

Lipi Mehta values little more than the written word. Her story, 'Twisted', was published in *Urban Shots: Love Collection*. She has also been the editor of a youth-oriented online magazine for two years and wishes to start a website of her own related to reading and its various facets.

URBAN SHOTS
YUVA

Edited by
Lipi Mehta

RUPA

Published by
Rupa Publications India Pvt. Ltd 2014
7/16, Ansari Road, Daryaganj
New Delhi 110002

Sales centres:
Allahabad Bengaluru Chennai
Hyderabad Jaipur Kathmandu
Kolkata Mumbai

ISBN: 978-81-291-2988-8

First impression 2014

10 9 8 7 6 5 4 3 2 1

The moral right of the author has been asserted.

To all the young writers out there
who aspire to tell beautiful stories.

Most of the stories in this collection are the shortlisted entries from the Mocha Grey Oak Urban Shots Competition 2012.

Special thanks to our Competition Partners—Mocha, Blog Adda, Helter Skelter and dfuse.in. We also thank the competition judges— R. Chandrasekar, Arun Kale, Sneh Thakur and Lipi Mehta.

Contents

Foreword

There's something that I do every time I meet someone who I want to get to know better—I make notes. People tend to call it 'passing judgments'; I look at it as 'case studies to understand human nature'. But mind you, this is not an active process that I choose for myself; honestly, I feel like a freak more often than not. But the deal is simple—it's essentially a post-it stuck in a part of my brain that is devoted to this little activity. Every time I meet an existing case study or one with seeming potential, the mental note-taking automatically starts. Nuances are noted, things that the subject itself might not know are seen by me and if I don't pen it down, it just stays there, accumulating what I believe is more clarity, with every interaction.

If I feel the need to, I compare notes with the concerned person. But more often than not, they're not ready to hear it. The fact remains that the story's been written and whoever decided to create this obsession in my head seems to have forgotten to provide an eraser. That's kind of how life is—sometimes, the narrator isn't who one thinks it is. And that's a truth better accepted than ignored.

It's often easier to think of how simple things were in our grandparents' or even parents' days, given the pace of life in current times. We're stuck—tangled up in this overly complicated web that is the present—and it only seems to get worse. But what we tend to forget is that sometimes, all we need is to reach the surface and breathe. Nothing more. Nothing less.

It's not easy to pen the unsaid things in one's life, things that have been forcefully drowned in silence by our subconscious or pushed out of our memory for some reason. But this book has managed to do just that—push one out of their comfort zone and into another's shoes, if only for a moment.

Written mostly by writers under the age of twenty-four, base emotions have been explored in these stories—varying from love, betrayal, confusion, lust, curiosity and of course, the one that makes for the most easily relatable stories—unhappiness. They allow a stranger to read between the lines and indulge in the past, present and future of the young writers, each one with a unique style of presenting their tale.

People from all walks of life are given a voice—from the taxi driver to the average college-going kid to the frustrated husband to the ice cream man whose profession is dying. The realistic nature of the characters, whether fictional or not, is hard to brush off, which one can interpret as signs of a story well told. There are, of course, instances of exaggeration and excess drama too, but that's nothing a willing suspension of disbelief won't let you enjoy.

Dreams that seem impossible are shown as possibilities. Bonds with forlorn family members are rekindled, societal norms are redefined and the joy of humanity is revived, even when disguised under layers of negativity and sarcasm. Legacies that pass down from generation to generation reflect how modernity has not rid India of its roots. In small and simple ways, there is an underlying optimism despite all the pessimism that society throws on you, the reader.

For those who have forgotten how to love, this book may just give a boost to reconsider the feeling or push you further away from the mere notion itself. It's the same with the spectrum of emotions that is brought out in these pages. In the end, the world of words is dependent on how one chooses to read it, based purely on individual perception backed by years and years, filtering out experiences. It's a mix of bittersweet feelings that lead you down memory lane sometimes, throwing you totally off course on others.

Treat it as fiction, or you might find parallels in this one. You are no different from the protagonists of the stories—you have your own dirty secrets, that one affair you thought nobody but the two of you knew about, bags full of regret that you tossed away into the deepest rivers of your mind praying that they would never resurface.

More importantly, read them as they were meant to be read—honest portrayals of incidents in a stranger's life that meant enough to them to write pages after pages about. Have an interesting journey through this book, meet the characters that are fleshed out and experience what they experienced. But please, don't try and rush towards the destination. Let the words take their time and do what they are supposed to.

Bon Voyage!
Rohini Kejriwal

Elephant

ADITHYA NARAYANAN

It began as a bright sunny Sunday morning but by the time the clock struck three, the clouds had turned grey and it slowly began drizzling outside. He had just finished lunch, and was lazing around, watching TV, when his eyes fell on the stack of photo albums lying on the sofa next to him, and he reached out to grab them. With half his mind on the business stories of the hour, he began flipping through the photos, paying little attention to them when suddenly a particular photograph caught his eye, and he flipped a page back to look at it again.

It was his junior high graduation class photograph, one of those pictures where the faces are so small that you can hardly make out one from another. The photo itself had been taken over a decade ago, and if you looked close enough, you could see a slight yellow tinge taking over the white of the paper.

His eyes immediately searched and fell upon a particular face in the photograph standing tall atop everybody else. He could immediately picture her in his head, on the day that the photograph was taken, her black hair shining in the heat of the summer sun.

His attention was deflected by the sound of his wife calling him from the other room.

He looked up from the album, but did not bother to reply. He'd been married to her for six years, long enough for him to know what it was about. She had probably misplaced some papers from work and wanted to ask him if he had seen them around, something she would eventually find herself under some files stacked up on her table, or somewhere within the depths of her bag, and so he went back to his album.

He couldn't take his eyes away from her face in the photograph and he continued staring at it, until his hands twitched and he began turning the pages of the album, hardly paying attention to the photographs, his mind now preoccupied with the flooding memories of years gone by.

His relationship with her had lasted for the last two years in college, and almost for a year after. After college, they had both decided to share a one-bedroom apartment in Dadar overlooking the main road, before he got admission in a business school that he had applied to. They had had a long discussion at the end of which they had decided to call their relationship off, and did so, the night before he left for London. It was a hard decision to make, but it made sense for them then, not to have the pressure or burden of a long distance relationship as they embarked upon their new and now separate lives. They kept in touch regularly for almost a year, until work took over for the both of them, and the phone calls died and slowly but surely, they drifted apart.

Life would go on, his parents moved back to Bangalore, and he met his wife at one of the family functions he attended on a trip back home. He got married to her three years later, much to the delight of both the families, and they moved to Bombay. He turned twenty-seven that November.

The two longest relationships of his life couldn't have been more in contrast with each other. In college, his relationship had been brash and unsteady. They had incessant squabbles, fights, and they'd broken up thrice before leaving college and then once more again before the final break-up.

His wife, on the other hand, was, and always had been the perfect Indian wife. She was independent, pretty and his parents loved the way she neatly plaited her hair. She played perfect host every time his friends came over and cooked the best dal makhani in town. She did her own things, went out with her girlfriends every Saturday afternoon to the movies and it looked like he couldn't have asked for a better married life.

But now, as he looked around his three-bedroom penthouse, he felt a sense of dullness and boredom taking over. Something in that one-bedroom apartment in Dadar had filled him with more than the three rooms in this house did. A sudden emptiness took over, and so strongly that he reached out for a glass of water on the table next to him, but it didn't quench his thirst.

Peace and quiet is good, but maybe love breeds better in an atmosphere of anger, fire and passion. At Dadar, they would yell, brawl and turn the house upside down. She would hit him, she had even slapped him once and they had thrown things at each other. But they would wake up the next morning to find their hands intertwined and would go about cleaning the house together before leaving for work. The people they met at parties, which they attended after work in the evenings, would find them perpetually next to each other, fingers interlinked throughout as they made their way around, exchanging pleasantries.

She understood him perfectly—his ways, his flaws, what he liked, what he didn't. Often he didn't have to speak to convey what he had on his mind; long nights were intersected with vast silences, often saying things that were deeper than what you would find in words of wisdom.

He looked up from the album, suddenly realized that he was going too far within his head into his past, and caught himself from drowning. He tried to reason with himself, it was pointless to look back. She was his ex-girlfriend, they had broken up over seven years ago and she would've made a lousy wife. She smoked a pack a day, said all the wrong things; he could've never taken her home to meet his parents. She hated cooking and the last time he saw her, she had cut her hair short in a way that would make his mother cry.

'Rahul!' screamed Swati again from the room next door, halting his flow of thought, and he could ignore her no longer. He placed the album on the top of the table and looked across the hall and saw her folding a pile of clothes. She wanted him to help her remove the clothes from outside as it was raining and they were getting wet. She hated it when that happened. He started to say something, but realized that she would not be able to hear him unless he yelled back, so decided against it.

After a couple of minutes of silence, he got up, walked across the hall, opened the door and walked out, bare feet and in his pyjamas, with his arms spread out in the rain.

ॐ

Long Walk Back to the Shore

AAKASH KARKARE

On that particular morning, Nikita awoke to a feeling she hadn't felt in a while—a sense of purpose. She lazily lifted her eyes to the clock directly in front of her and noticed it was only 6.30. Some rays of sunlight fell into her eyes from the window adjacent to the bed. She yawned, stretched out her arms and turned over to avoid them. She was about to fall asleep again when she remembered why she felt this way. It was her wedding anniversary—seventeenth overall and first since Sahil, her husband had died—and she had decided to celebrate their anniversary all by herself.

Nikita took a long, hot shower. The water calmed her and she felt all her worries and troubles slowly leave her. She felt completely empty and relaxed when she was done with her shower. She stood in front of the mirror on her cupboard door for a while. She imagined Sahil standing next to her.

She imagined him running his hands through her hair and grinning like he used to. For a while she was filled with warmth but then she remembered that it was all a fantasy. Sadness began filling every pore in her body so she quickly got dressed and went to the kitchen. Focusing on daily activities helped her forget the pain, albeit momentarily. In the kitchen she equipped herself with a bottle of Old Monk, a tray of ice cubes and a glass. She carried all of this into the living room and plopped herself down on the couch.

This was how Nikita and Sahil had begun their wedding anniversaries for the past sixteen years. Sahil with his rum and Nikita with her beer but today was all about Sahil and what he liked. The Old Monk had been a hangover from Sahil's college days; he had called it the 'fastest and cheapest way to get drunk'. She lined the glass with four ice cubes. She poured the rum into the glass until it was half full and then downed it in one go. It was horrible. Her eyes began watering and there was a terrible taste in her mouth. She felt nauseous. She popped an ice cube into her mouth and sucked on it for a while. It got rid of the awful taste and subdued her nausea. Her mother had gotten her into the habit; she would give her an ice cube to suck on as a treat if she ate her greens. She selected *Casablanca* from the huge DVD collection that she and Sahil had accumulated over the years and popped it into the player. The credits began to roll and she leaned back on the couch while hugging a pillow to enjoy the film.

Nikita had first seen *Casablanca* when she was sixteen at a film club in college and had instantly fallen in love with it. The film had filled her heart with a swirl of emotions and it was the first film that had made her cry. She hadn't been able to take part in the post-film discussion where a bunch of people had called it outdated and unrealistic. In her eyes those people had been stupid and they had made her feel alienated. She had drifted out of the classroom in a daze and had walked home in rapture. Years later, about six months into their relationship when Sahil had said that *Casablanca* was his favourite film, she knew she was going to marry him.

Nikita was sucked into the movie when Bogart's Rick first

entered the scene. For her it was the greatest film ever made and she began to enjoy the things she had always enjoyed. The music, the dialogues, Ingrid Bergman, Peter Lorre and of course, Humphrey Bogart. After some time however, she began to lose interest. She knew how it would end. She knew what would happen to all the characters and what they would say to each other. All those years of watching the film with Sahil had elevated it to some other level. Now without him the film seemed very pointless. For a while she forced herself to continue watching it. But all it did was remind her that she was watching the film all alone. Nikita turned off the television, threw away the remaining rum and drank a glass of water before heading to the bedroom. She stared at her unmade bed for a while and then crawled in.

After the movie Sahil and Nikita would head back to the bedroom and spend most of the afternoon having sex and whatever remained of it, taking a nap in each other's arms. Today, for a while she just lay in bed and stared at the ceiling; in the ceiling she saw all those afternoons they had spent together. They seemed decades away—as if they hadn't happened at all. There was a picture of Sahil on the bedside table. She picked it up and looked at it. He was smiling a little sheepishly at the camera as he always did when he was posing. Slowly she slipped her free hand under the covers and into her jeans and began masturbating. She imagined a naked Sahil. She imagined their lovemaking. Nothing was happening. She was too aware of what she was doing. She increased the tempo of her hands but she didn't feel anything, let alone bringing herself to orgasm. The guy in the picture didn't look like Sahil. She had forgotten how he looked. In her memories there was a blur where his face had been but it wasn't the guy in the photo. She removed her hand and replaced the photograph on the table.

She felt an intense sense of frustration. She felt like screaming to release the anger and pain. Hot tears began rolling down her cheeks. It had been a horrible year for her. She hadn't left the house and had just drowned in her own sorrow. Suicide had been contemplated many times. She couldn't go on living like this—alternating between numbness and pain. In her mind this anniversary celebration was an attempt to say goodbye—to confront all those emotions and then let them go. She let herself continue crying. She ran out of tears and began feeling calm, completely empty of emotion. Tired from her ordeal she fell asleep.

She woke up refreshed after a four-hour nap. She was lying on her stomach and the bed sheet near her face was wet with tears and drool. She dragged herself out of bed and walked into the kitchen. She saw the supermarket bag lying on the table. In this part of the day, Sahil and Nikita would cook a nice gourmet meal together—a new recipe from an old cooking book Nikita's mom had gifted them. Today was pasta primavera with white wine and tiramisu. She couldn't bring herself to do any cooking. She quietly went to the shelves in the corner and pulled out a packet of Maggi and began cooking it. She threw in a slice of cheese and some red chilli powder. She poured herself a glass of orange juice and sat down at the table to enjoy her simple meal.

The food fortified her and she became a little relaxed. The air of melancholy that had hung over her, lifted. The Maggi made her realize how hungry she was. She started making the pasta from the recipe book. For a while she didn't think of anything else except preparing it. She cut up the vegetables and the pieces of meat, boiled the pasta and transferred all the ingredients to a pan where butter and garlic sizzled away. She worked like a well-oiled machine and focused on nothing but the task at hand. The pasta was delicious. Every warm, cheesy bite made her a little happier.

As she was shovelling it into her mouth, she began recalling all the happy times Sahil and she had spent cooking their anniversary dinner. But in these happy reminisces slipped a niggle of doubt. She began thinking if all these times had happened at all. It all felt like a dream. Sahil seemed to have never existed at all. The will to continue eating left her. She threw away the remaining pasta.

They had ended their anniversary days with a trip to Marine Drive on Sahil's father's scooter with a sidecar. It was one of those old Bajaj scooters that you didn't see on the roads anymore. Sahil would sit in the sidecar on the way to Marine Drive and Nikita would sit in the sidecar on the way back. In between they would sit at Chowpatty for a while and enjoy some kulfi. Nikita went down to the garage of her building and walked towards the scooter. The sidecar had been detached a long time ago and lay in a corner gathering dust. She got onto the scooter, turned the key in the ignition, kicked the starter and set off for Marine Drive.

Nikita let her hair fly in the wind. She reached Chowpatty and parked it. She bought herself a malai kulfi and then sat on the sand to enjoy it. She licked it until she couldn't lick it anymore. She swallowed the remaining piece hanging onto the stick and then threw it away. She just lay there in the sand for a while and played with her hair. She didn't think of anything in particular. Scenes from her life came into her mind and went away. She tried to remember the last time Sahil and she had come to Chowpatty. After Sahil's death her life was divided into two parts—pre-Sahil and post-Sahil. She didn't know what to do with herself. At forty-two, she had to start all over again. Find something new to do, create a new life. It was like being twenty again. She felt that uncertainty and doubt again. The feeling of being lost in an alien world. She got up and walked to the scooter.

It spluttered to a start and she began driving slowly along the promenade. Halfway down the promenade, the scooter halted and refused to go any further. She pushed it and tried to kick-start it a couple of times but it refused to budge. She would have to call a tow truck. She stood up and reached into her pocket and was about to dial the number but in that moment the whole day came up in front of her. All day long she had tried to recreate the past but none of the things had gone right. All it had done was remind her that she could not recreate it. A feeling of repulsion came over her when she stared down at the scooter. She had to let go of it, the memories and the past. Otherwise, she would have to kill herself. But she didn't want to do that. In her mind's eye she saw herself standing in the centre of the sea. The past was like the waves trying to pull her into the sea and drown her in its vastness. In the fallen scooter she saw Sahil and everything else she had been refusing to let go of. Slowly, she began walking away from the scooter. With each step she took away from it, she saw herself inching closer to the shore. She hailed a taxi and sat in it. The driver started the meter and began driving away to her house. A popular song began playing on the radio. Nikita saw the waves receding away from her and back into the abyss they had come from. A wry smile played on her lips as she joined the driver in singing the song on the radio.

ॐ

Bittersweet

NAOMI SARAH

Ria was tired of meeting men she couldn't have. They were either complex, confused, chaotic, cruel or cheaters. Smiling cynically, she realized the words that best described these men began with the letter 'c'. How messed up.

There was a knock on the door—she instinctively knew it was him. He was the only one who never rang the doorbell upon arrival. Quickly, she lit a cigarette and made her way to the door, running her fingers swiftly through her slightly damp hair. She liked it when he came home just after she'd showered—she smelled divine.

As soon as the door was open, a pleasant warmth invaded her chest travelling straight to her toes. Instead of offering him a smile she punched him in the side. 'Why are you late...again?' she demanded, pretending to look mad. She was, in truth, used to him being late.

'What's wrong with you? I stopped to buy you a pack of smokes,' he said, giving her a look that said he thought she was crazy. 'Still, you were supposed to be here twenty minutes ago,' she replied, walking over to the couch, plonking herself down while reaching for the ashtray. She watched him remove his jacket slowly as he looked over at the television screen to see which movie was on.

'Alright fine, I'm sorry your highness. So, how's it going?' he asked, glancing at her briefly before lighting a cigarette, seating himself next to her. Her limbs immediately made themselves comfortable as she snuggled up to him. It was bizarre how naturally her body welded itself against his frame.

'The usual stuff. Interviews, freelance work, stress...'

Her voice trailed off as she looked up at him. He always wore a keen expression while he listened to her.

'What about you? How was the wedding on Saturday?'

'Nothing fancy, really. Relatives pestering me about when I'll get married, mom nudging me towards a girl who barely looked older than twenty—I managed to slip away though.' He sighed and took a deep drag from his cigarette. Ria looked away from him. She hated the fact that he still had an effect on her even when they were talking about the insignificant.

She'd known him for almost two years and remembered how the kindness in his voice had lured her. She met him by chance and was thankful their paths had crossed. She liked how he always cleared his throat midway through a sentence and how he would absent-mindedly draw invisible patterns on her thigh as he spoke.

The men she met were bad boys who spat profanity and always had a malicious way about them. She met nice guys too who later emerged from their cocoons as complete jerks. And here was a guy who was the epitome of all that was painfully sweet and kind-hearted. She was attracted to a man who wasn't even her type.

Sometimes he would anger her with his indifference towards the small details she cared about—God, how she hated how he never fought back with a similar fierceness. Their arguments were heated from her end, but subdued on his. She admired yet loathed his tensile patience.

He was engrossed in the movie *Something's Gotta Give*, laughing heartily when Diane Keaton gets caught stark naked in the hallway by Jack Nicholson. Sliding down, she lay on his lap looking towards the screen but not really watching. She wasn't in love with him, but she cared immensely. There were days she missed him terribly but didn't dare to say it out loud.

Theirs was a complicated arrangement—no strings attached and no emotional baggage. The rules were simple and she knew deep down that it was never going to be more than an 'arrangement'. He was Muslim and she, Hindu. Need she say more? Besides, he was the pious kind of Muslim—maintained a fast every Ramadan, went for prayers, didn't drink or do drugs. Boring! He was surely better off without the vices because somehow it made him pure and untainted in an odd yet relieving way.

It deeply upset her to think of the day that would inevitably arrive when they would go their separate ways. He was being shoved towards the pit of marriage while struggling not to fall in (at least not for now) and he was considering leaving the city and returning to his home town. Sigh. They were poles apart and yet she couldn't imagine life without his gentle and infuriating ways.

'I'm hungry. Let's eat already,' he said, moving her away as he got up from the sofa, making a beeline for the kitchen.

She'd cooked for him that morning and was hoping the meal she'd painstakingly prepared was good. He was extremely picky about which spices and herbs went into a dish. She often told him how she already pitied his future wife.

She ushered him out of the kitchen and got busy putting his plate together, reheating the dish on the burner. While she waited for it to sizzle to life, he came from behind and wrapped his arms tightly around her waist, planting a kiss on her cheek. God damn him, her heart was starting to palpitate.

Pulling herself together she cried, 'Go outside and wait! Seriously, before I burn you with this hot spoon!'

Grinning to reveal a set of teeth that set off his alarmingly cute smile, he trotted back into the hall leaving her frowning. Lifting two plates out of the kitchen, she made her way into the living room. Ria watched in rapt attention from next to him as he took his first morsel and chomped hungrily.

'This tastes good,' he said approvingly, kissing her on the cheek again before turning back to the television. Damn it, that intoxicating yet harmless kiss. She heaved a sigh of relief and began eating as well, grateful that there was no blunt criticism about the meal. He could be brutally honest when it came to her cooking, even if it was just tea or coffee she was preparing.

After he was done eating he returned from the kitchen and sat contentedly next to her while lighting his second cigarette, offering her another. She sat silently on one end of the sofa observing him. He didn't notice her peering at him so intently, so ruefully. The smoke from their cigarettes filled the void between them, as she continued to stare through the poisonous haze. She thought about how she was going to tell him that the arrangement was over. How she was sure that this time, was the final time that they were to ever be at that kind of proximity.

Glancing her way, he reached out to pull her towards him—she reluctantly got cosy against his warm body. Almost immediately, time was at a standstill. She took a deep breath, her heart almost breaking at the realization that she was mentally saving his scent for a rainy day. She wanted to visually gorge every bit of him. His strong arms, his vanilla skin, his ecru eyes. Aching from a part inside her, she held back tears to disguise her anguish.

Sitting up straight but not moving away from his side, she stubbed her cigarette a little after he snuffed his. She'd already told him that they needed to discuss the mess and stomp it underfoot before it raged into something uncontrollable. The difference between them was that he was a master at hiding his emotions and not letting it surface. She, on the other hand, was afraid she would react like a child being told that her parents died in a car crash.

He finally noticed her staring at him, uncomfortably shifting his gaze back to the television, clearing his throat. He finally spoke. 'Why do you have to be so bloody dramatic? Things were going fine. We always have the same discussion and end up fighting like rabid dogs. Well you, at least.' He added the last bit with half a smile, aware that her look meant the discussion was on.

'I know. But it's getting to me. I can't keep up with the pretence. You and I both know that it'll be harder to end this, years from now. It's not right to think that this is normal to continue.' She was looking down at her hands, averting her eyes from his piercing gaze.

He sighed audibly, running his fingers through his hair, undecided about what to say next. Sometimes she wanted to see the pain in his eyes too, to witness a shadow of misery that he often saw cloaking hers. Instead he drew her closer, kissing her with a softness that felt like a dove's wings beating against her lips. Pushing him away, she could've sworn she glimpsed wreckage in his eyes. But it was put out like a candle in a gust of wind and she was enveloped with another kiss that could only be described as transcendental. She could wait for another day to have her heart ripped out.

☙❦❧

Our Sunday

TNAHSIN GARG

Today was one of those wretched days that obliged me to pick my journal at night and pour selected memories down, before I descended into slumber with a heavy heart. Although I may not be able to dwell upon the intricacies of today's events (as I have to wake up early for office tomorrow morning), I shall try to tell as much as I can or at least as much as I should.

We woke up at noon, as is usually the case on Sunday mornings, not due to the fact that we stayed up late the previous night, which isn't true in the first place (as *that* rarely happened), but perhaps because, we weren't really ready to embrace the fact that the weekend was almost over and we hadn't finished whatever extraneous chores and leisurely entertainments we had planned. I stretched myself and then shrunk beneath the comforter like an innocent but lazy school boy when I heard the noise of the running shower coming from our bathroom and tried to save some of the dream I believed I still had in my vision. But no, the sweet dream melted away, and I soon found myself rubbing my eyes, pulling my lanky frame upright, and scanning the floor with my bare feet in search of my slippers. Not even a moment had passed and she emerged from the bathroom, wrapped in many white long towels covering herself almost entirely. Hiding herself from *me!*

When I asked her if there was any possibility that she could join me back in the bed she was quick to refuse, and said something like, '…the weekend quota is over.' Actually, she said a lot of other things in addition but I can't write them down here. It'll be foolish to whine about *that* because it's very normal and I suppose (rather, I hope) that these kinds of regular refusals to a poor husband's basic needs occur everywhere in the world. And if not, then I'm doomed.

Also, as I said, this journal entry can't possibly explain everything about our relationship (you may have to read the entire journal for that, not that I ever intend to share it), thus I shall quicken the pace of my narration. After that quick refusal, I grunted something which she kindly ignored, and then walking into the dressing room, she declared the schedule for our Sunday. *Our* Sunday, she clarified through repetition. I had always thought it was *my* Sunday. But after my parents tied me into this holy knot a few months ago, several things had changed. Sundays and holidays were just the minorities amongst the aspects of my life that were victimized by this kind and beloved lady in my life.

She announced that we were first going to visit the mall for *some* shopping. After all the time that I have spent shopping with her, I haven't really understood what 'some' constitutes or exactly refers to. But the horrors that this word 'some' brings before my eyes are as fresh as any morning tea that a loving wife provides her husband every day (not that I am asking you to infer that mine is not a lovely wife or that I am not provided by such a tea—it's just that this journal's privacy may be compromised in future by the very person about whom it's often written and maintained, and if such is the case, I would like to take this opportunity to make it very clear to that very same person that I love her beyond anything and all this that I have written so far is merely a silly act, a false drama, an endless farce, which might get published someday, although against my will, and somehow in the favour of my wealth and fortune, which I will ultimately sprinkle upon her, oh dearest, sweetest wife!)

And after we were done with *some* shopping, my wife continued reciting the routine while disrupting my insignificant train of thought, *we* would stop by at the grain market, and get some much-needed groceries. But *of course*, she stressed the last syllables while straightening out a stubborn lock of hair, we would only *stop by* and not spend more time than we usually do. And then, when the day's spent perfectly ('perfect' being defined according to her own unbiased preference), we would have dinner at that place we discovered accidentally last time we went out, whose name she presently can't remember but that very same one she said she really loved, and where I made faces and complained about the spices. I realize now that I shouldn't have told her the name when she pressed me, but being the kind creature that I am, I told her immediately on seeing her distressed, and felt proud for showing off my skilled and learned memory but soon felt rather like a loser who had accidentally pulled the trigger of the pistol that lay tucked safely in his own pants. Yes, we did go to that place for dinner, and no, I did not like the food there, and yes, this didn't matter to her much, and no, she hasn't forgotten the name of the place since, and yes, it's very likely that now we'll go there every week, and no, I still haven't applied for a divorce.

When all was said and done (I'm again skipping some details of the ordained hectic schedule), I felt as if I needed to raise my little finger up in the air to seek a permission to speak or to make a humble request, especially judging by the way she was looking down at me, expecting me to be as obedient as I have always been since the beginning of time. But it was different this time, it was very different, it wasn't just any common holiday. It was India's first match in the World Cup. Now, now, now, do I even *need* to say more?

I mean, it's self-evident at this point. We all know in whose favour the blind balance of justice should tip. Yes, I agree that perhaps in all these months she couldn't quite notice my passion for sport and Sachin, and just tagged me merely as a medium grade, obedient husband—a tag that usually lasts a lifetime. But then, isn't this passion for cricket, that's reserved for men, too well-known and too well-established to be ignored in the first place? Do we not know that for women shopping is akin to making love (and sometimes even superior)? Then how is it that our needs are not considered or brought into the right light? No, not fair, not fair.

The little finger that rose in the air was crushed like a stone under a bulldozer, the humble voice that originated from my throat, no, from my *heart* was muted like a TV channel with a flick of a remote, the fiery passion that once, no not once, many a time rose in my soul was left unfulfilled like an unwanted shrub, denied water and left alone to dry and die.

And thus, we did whatever she wanted in whichever way she preferred, and the Sunday swept away like dust on floor, with me left relying on the highlights of the match to be shown tomorrow. But the story doesn't end here. I didn't intend to share my suffering and sorrow, because that's something quite commonplace in my life, and if I went at lengths of narrating it every single day, God knows how many journals I would need. It's about the occasional bliss that strikes upon my life by chance; that very momentous bliss did come on this Sunday, rather Sun-night, when, tired from our day's hectic schedule I was lying on my bed in routine pajamas, and she appeared from the dressing room in one of those rare flimsy, low-neck gowns that I know that she had secured in her closet long since but hardly ever wore them.

I could see it on her face, in her eyes to be exact, that fixed gaze of hers slightly imbued with passion, and fully enveloped in a naughty indulgence that at once left me wounded yet mad with thrill. Somehow she had perceived my long suffering in the course of the day, and knew how exactly she could make it up to me in a matter of few minutes. And *that*, she did.

Presently, she's sleeping right next to me as I scribble these words. Oh, how sweetly does she breathe from her bosom, and how tenderly does that lock of hair lie on her quivering lip! But I can't touch her now, lest she wakes up to be cross with me. I too am nodding with the burden of sleep after this occasional performance, and now I must lie down, next to her. What a fine Sunday it was! Did I call it wretched in the beginning? I am a fool if I did. Anyway, tomorrow is Monday, let's see what it's got in store for me, I mean, for *us*.

Gifts From America

KAILASH SRINIVASAN

The phone rang at three in the morning, cutting through the stillness of the night with the brutality of a chainsaw. They ignored the shrill ringing like a bad dream, but it continued to ring. If one had the knack to decipher between types of phone rings, they would know it was an international call, the kind with long beeps. Balu's family had several relatives for whom home meant the United States.

Balu's father usually slept at 9:30 every night and believed any calls made after that should only be for nuclear emergencies. He woke up at 4.00 a.m. to tend to his plants and go for a walk in his ironed tracksuit. Presently, he got up with a start, slapping his wife's arm, and in the process, alarming her.

'Who is it? Who is it?' he cried now, flailing his arms and opening his glassy, red eyes.

'How am I supposed to know?' Balu's mother replied. 'Answer it, answer the damn thing,' she said.

He turned the light on and picked it up after the eighth ring.

'Annadaan pesurain,' said a husky voice of a man. 'It's me.'

He was too impatient to be polite and made clear his vexation. 'What now? You expect me to guess who you are at three in the morning?'

'Aiyo, were you sleeping? Sorry, sorry,' said the man.

'Of course not. We generally don't sleep at night. We were singing bhajans. Want to join?'

Balu's mother tapped his arm to inquire who it was but he ignored her.

'Aiyo, very sorringey. Been here all my life and I still don't understand this time difference business. We all live on the same planet, no?'

'Who is this?' he asked irritably.

'Sunderashekharan here,' the man said, a hint of a bruised ego in his voice. 'You don't recognize my voice, Mani?'

'Yes, I do. Let me hand the phone to Lakshmi,' he said quickly, giving her a look as he did so, with the full knowledge that there would be retorts: *when your family calls I should be all proper and smile, but when my family calls, you make faces?*

After nodding for almost everything and getting the leeway to only speak in monosyllables, she hung up, and went to turn off the light.

'Let it be, no. We might as well get up and go about our day. It's almost morning.'

'Okay, okay enough with the taunts. They are calling from New York. I can't be rude, no?'

'Aama, periya New York. Big deal. Bloody moron, is what he is. Can't get his head around time difference and has the nerve to tell me that.'

'He called to inform that they are coming to India and will visit us.'

'Oh, such an honour, I feel so blessed.'

Ignoring that remark, she said, 'They missed Balu's Poonal, no. He was saying how bad he felt for not making it.'

'Bullshit. That miser would have come had I told him I'd reimburse his flight tickets. I know that man very well.'

'What nonsense! Nothing like that. You always misunderstand my family. Something important must have come up. Anyway, they are arriving next week.'

'Is it? Lovely.'

'Hmph!' she said. 'I'll go and tell Balu. He'll be so excited.'

Balu was flopped on his stomach, snoring rhythmically. His mother gently called out his name once or twice. He didn't budge. She sat next to him and shook him slightly by his shoulder.

'Yennamaa, what is it?' he said impatiently and covered his face with the sheet.

'Your mama-thathais coming from New York.'

'Rombamukyon. Was this a matter of life and death that it couldn't wait till morning?'

His mother rose from her position and bringing her brows together said, 'You also like your father, are just as indifferent. No one cares in this house that my beloved uncle is coming to visit us.'

It had always baffled Balu, these dual titles, amma-ma and chithi-patti and what not. Balu lay awake, struggling to understand his connection to this mama-thatha from New York. But the discomfort of being awoken in mid-sleep was assuaged by a tinge of excitement, the expectation of receiving an expensive gift, maybe an iPod, or the new iPad? He couldn't wait to have one of his own.

The day arrived dousing the entire house with an air of anticipation, especially his mother, who couldn't stand still. She went all out in making the house look spotless, like orphanages prepare when they know some prospective fair-skinned parents are visiting from abroad. The best face had to be put up. No one was to move an inch till the maid had mopped the floor and it had dried appropriately. She warned them against stepping on the wet floor and leaving footprints all over.

No one was to sit on the couch or on any of the beds covered with brand new sheets. If they wished to sit, Nilkamal plastic chairs were their best option. It seemed to Balu that his mother wanted him to monitor even his breathing, lest he exhaled rather forcefully and spoiled the set-up of the house.

'Which car does Mani drive?' Balu's mama-thatha had asked a day before he was to arrive, further fuelling his father's hatred for the man. 'You see, I don't understand this small car fascination of the Indian middle class.'

'Tell him to catch a bloody taxi,' he'd replied, but went to the airport anyway to pick his wife's relatives.

At home, Balu's mother was listing all the possible gifts that she thought might soon adorn her house, or perhaps jewellery to titivate her neck, her ears, even. Maybe, American dollars. *Rama, this excitement will kill me.* Balu, she was hoping, would get maybe a nice watch. *I have to show that Gomathi mami for once. Break her proud nose. Can't wait to tell her, I too have gifts from America. And better than her stupid perfume bottles and chocolates her son sends from California.*

She looked around one last time to make sure everything was in place. The bell sounded and she rushed to the door to welcome her America-bred mama and mami. They got in, dumped their huge bags and collapsed on the couch.

'What pollution, rama, rama. What impatient drivers, plus the heat. No air conditioning in the car, no. Mani, it's time to buy a new car.'

Why don't you buy me one? Mani wanted to say, but instead went with 'Hmm'.

Mama-thatha scratched his bald pate and opened two buttons of his half-sleeved shirt to let some air in. The inner vest that was now peeking out was far from being white. He made a face when he looked around and found no air conditioner. His wife, who was twice his size, the size of a drum wound with a silk sari around it, was wheezing after having to take the stairs. She proudly claimed that lifts never went out of order in America.

Now she was gesturing wildly, as her words were buried under her deep-throated breathing. Lakshmi took some time to interpret them, eventually figuring out that she was asking for a glass of water. For the rest of the day Lakshmi kept glancing at the big suitcases that had come with the NRIs, but they had no inclination to open them. *Maybe they will hand over all those wonderful presents first thing in the morning,* she thought.

It was Mami's third tumbler of coffee. Lakshmi brought it over.

'So, how did the Poonal go?' Mami asked.

This was Lakshmi's golden chance to steer the conversation in the direction she wanted.

'Oh, it was a very nice ceremony, went well. Balu got so many gifts, it was too much. People brought silk saris for me and silk veshtis for Balu's father also.'

'Tch! We missed it. What happened you know? Last-minute plan it was, really. Our friends wanted us to come to Europe. We have so many friends, you know. They had us fly in business class and all.'

'Well, that's nice. Okay, let me ask Balu to say abhivadiye and do namaskaram.'

'Ah, yes, yes. Yenanga, the child wants our blessings.'

Lakshmi thought if the gift is in cash, it would be no less than ten thousand rupees. After all it is not a big sum for them. The gifts will come later. She waited for her mama to make a move and get his wallet. But what added to her anxiety was the man's complete lack of movement. His wife barked her instructions few more times, but he just sat there with the paper in his hands.

'I think you should gargle with lukewarm water,' said Lakshmi. 'Maybe your voice is not audible enough for him.'

By now Balu's father too was feverish with anticipation. He'd asked Lakshmi in bed last night whether he might get a GPS navigation system for his car and she'd winked.

It took one more growl to rouse Mama from his position. He returned with a small pouch and stood to his wife's right side. Lakshmi thought it was perhaps gold coins or a diamond ring.

'Balu, come, come, hurry up.' He had just come out of his bath wrapping a silk veshti around his waist. The freshly smeared holy ash on his forehead, chest and arms was still drying. A bright red dot of vermillion stood between his eyebrows.

'Ah hah, ah hah, look at that glowing face,' Mami said to her husband, swaying her head now left, now right. 'Murugaa,'she sang.

Balu placed his palms next to his ears, and with a bowed head, said abhivadiye and followed it with a sashtanganamaskaram, fully prostrating in front of the elders. Mama and Mami blessed him by showering him with turmeric-dyed rice and wishes for his bright future. Then arrived the moment that Balu and family had been waiting for. Mama-thatha slowly undid the small pouch and with the generous flourish of a king, drew out a note. Balu's family froze in mid-gasp.

Slowly, the man unfolded a note, weary and beyond its youth. A note so old, Lakshmi thought it possibly was the first one issued by the government of India. The old man and woman then held the note together and handed it over to Balu as though it were a family heirloom. When held against the light, Balu found nearly seventy-eight holes in the fifty-rupee note. He looked over his shoulder at his mother, his father. His shoulders sank as he made a retreat.

The NRI couple settled in their chairs and a curious Mami asked Lakshmi, 'So, what do you think he's going to spend that money on?'

Balu's father rising from his seat now, said in a clear voice, 'Maybe he will use it to book your business class tickets back to New York.'

The Travelling Autowallah

ESHA VAISH

Gangaram opened the fraying incense stick packet and removed two of them. Holding them in his grubby fingers he lit them and the aroma of rose hit his nostrils. The PMC had cut water in his settlement and Gangaram was revealed smelling something other than the sweat that he reeked of. In front of him was a photo of Ganpati and a world map. Gangaram smiled to himself even as his lips began muttering his own concocted prayer. If his conservative father had been alive, Gangaram knew that the old man would have given him a beating. He wouldn't have approved of the world map glued next to the Ganpati photo, stains of grease and others lining its creases. Neither would he have approved of Gangaram's prayers. Gangaram wasn't a believer in equality for all religions, neither did he care. His prayer, a garbled mix of English, Hindi, Urdu and German wasn't to appease any God, it was so that his dream would come true, his dream of travelling the world.

As far back as Gangaram could remember he had only wanted this. He had grown up without the money to buy any frills. His father worked hard as an autowallah, putting Gangaram through school. However, as strange as destiny is, Gangaram hated school. He preferred Sundays when his father would take him to work and he would sit on the corner of a threadbare cushion and enjoy every bump on the road. The bumps were craters and often going over one, Gangaram would be suspended in the air for a few seconds, landing with a painful thud, but he didn't mind. His mind didn't register the pain as he was enthralled by the winding roads that spread out across him, the network of messy lanes, the manoeuvring around old men on bicycles and paan shop dustbins on the road that he could see through the rickshaw's clear front glass.

So when Gangaram failed the seventh standard for the fourth time, believing that persistent failure would weaken his strict father's resolve to see him an educated man, he got his way. With his love for travel, destiny took its intended course and Gangaram took to his father's rickshaw profession. However, even as Gangaram found peace in his new job, he drove his father to an early grave. Seeing his only son (who was followed by a string of girls, till the doctor declared the wife unfit of producing another) want nothing more from his life, his father lost his only reason to live. He took to drinking. One night, two bottles of whisky and the Mula-Mutha delivered him to his afterlife. Gangaram mourned, more for his widowed mother's sake than his own. His three unmarried sisters mourned for the dowry that would never be and the three married ones counted their lucky stars that their thresholds remained unmarked by his death. As the dutiful son, Gangaram took up the mantle as the family head for the next three years and deposited 15,000 rupees dowry to be divided amongst the three sisters. His mother gave him her blessing laced generously with tears and Gangaram, the ever dutiful son accepted them with his head slightly bowed. He wondered, would she have felt this way had she known that the money hadn't come from solely driving a rickshaw, but had been heavily subsidized by his side businesses. However, secrets are the glue that holds families together and Gangaram's was no different. He vowed this one would go to the grave with him.

With money, proposals poured in. Young men searching for money to squander on khambas of desi and flesh to dig in when they got back were found in dozens in the slums. Gangaram handpicked the three scrawniest men out of the lot and married off his sisters. At least, he thought, if the men took to domestic abuse, his sisters would survive the strokes from these massless, scrawny vermin.

Everything in his life settled, Gangaram washed his hands of his dubious side businesses and thus began his longest love affair with travel. He travelled the length and breadth of the city, taking passengers where no autowallah dared, sleeping in dingy alleys, speeding up on highways and taking illegal turns. It was a high-paced life and Gangaram savoured every moment of it. Marriage came along the way, but neither the wedding night nor the birth of his first son could indulge him in anything more than niceties. He was neither shackled by the marriage nor perturbed by it, for his heart thumped in sync only to the hum of his rickshaw engine.

Eventually, the thrill wore off. The sights in his mirror turned banally familiar and Gangaram began seeking with the desperation of a traveller, newer places to conquer. When his eyes had turned sore and vacant, and his legs had grown used to braking on all the familiar potholes, Gangaram had an epiphany. No, he realized. He was not a man to be chained to the roads of one city, to live a stagnated life; he was going to be the man to drive his rickshaw across the globe. If Gangaram had paid attention in Geography till the seventh, he might have realized the continents weren't a fused mass, but sparsely decorated across oceans. However, the innocent dreams of an illiterate man had taken birth in his mind and they grew like a virus. Gangaram found himself consumed by the thrill of leaving Pune, but he was no fool. He realized that he needed money, a plan and perhaps even some knowledge.

So, he did what he knew best. He drove through the lanes of Koregaon Park, their calm, green atmosphere transporting him to an alternate reality. He felt they were a different city, with their eclectic mix of coloured and white people, where even the Indians spoke Hindi strangely. Gangaram credited that moment of lucidity to his life from that point. He realized he needed to befriend foreigners and learn more to be prepared when he travelled to the world outside Pune.

Thus began Gangaram's alternate education. He was a sincere student, always loitering around the area, seeking the most vulnerable passengers, stalkerishly watching the way their lips moved as strange sounds and syllables pieced together resonated around them and even meticulously maintaining diary entries of any information he learned and deemed useful. It became such an obsession that Gangaram found himself wanting to be more and more 'glo-cal' as the *Amreekans* had called it, a local meant for global exploits is the way he comprehended it.

One day, he was driving around a particularly roguish German man. Some of his customers were outright rude and some were friendly. This German ended up being of the latter sorts. En route Baner to Koregaon Park, he entertained Gangaram's questions and when they reached German Bakery, the place the foreigner wanted to go, Gangaram felt a pang of sadness seeing the blonde man leave. He smiled at him when he gave him his fare and bid him goodbye with a wave of his hand. The man might have found Gangaram's temperament curious, but like most foreigners his excitement over being in India overruled his better judgement to not indulge strangers.

Gangaram started the rickshaw and began driving off. Halfway through, an object in the back seat caught his eye. It was a bag, a sling bag with the word 'Ram' plastered on every square inch. Alarmed that the man might miss his bag, Gangaram begun turning his vehicle around, almost colliding with a crazy two-wheeler rider. He yelled the appropriate number of customary abuses, sticking his head out and yelling much after the young boy had zipped past. It was a road tradition and a habit moreover. With that, he swung his rickshaw around and trudged along the pockmarked road. He hadn't gotten very far and Germany Bakery made an appearance. Unlike the hype that surrounded it, the place had a very unassuming demeanour which was not unusual for all the brilliant landmarks in Pune slung around quietly, coaxing travellers to seek them out rather than declaring themselves with wood and steel.

Gangaram's rickshaw grunted to a stop across the road. Nodding to the fellow hawkers and indulging in some street gossip born more out of familiarity than interest, he requested them to look after his rickshaw before crossing the road with the bag in his hand. His head buzzed with a number of questions that he would ask the man. Perhaps this German man would be his golden find, helping him to lay his groundwork for his world travels.

Hrishikesh stared at the man looking back at him from the cover. His oily hair perfectly combed into two halves giving way to a large forehead and a stout nose. The outline of a moustache that had no business on his face lurked above his angry and swollen upper lip, even swallowing the lower one as it graciously rolled over. Gangaram Sathe, his father, whom Hrishikesh knew more about than the picture revealed.

Yet, he bowed his head in reverence and said, 'Baba, you're

finally touring the world. I told you one day I'd make it happen.'
This vow, that had led Hrishikesh across several continents talking
about his late father's bestseller, *The Travelling Autowallah*, that had
made him take the scrawny pages of his father's dairy from his
rickshaw and slave over it through many litres of gasoline, which
had given him the strength to write to publishers and put all his
other aspirations on hold, had been born the day he was a seven-
year-old boy whose father had been claimed by a twist of fate. For
many months after that, his mother cried every time they moved
past the big gaping hole at the corner of Koregaon Park's Lane 1.
It was all over the news, the German Bakery blast, and his father
had been just a number in the seventeen who lost their lives.

When the funeral procession turned a blurred memory,
Hrishikesh found himself spending more and more time with his
inheritance—a lone rickshaw. The key to the compartment in the
front was missing, having turned a molten rock with his father's
charred body. One day in an outburst of sorrow, he broke through
it with a hammer, yelling at the inanimate object, everything his
father should have been around to hear. In the debris he created,
Hrishikesh found an answer, not the one he had hoped for but it
was a start. It was a pocket book, a cloth and glue binding over
cardboard sheets; it looked like the book kiranawallahs used to
maintain monthly tallies. Hrishikesh lifted it delicately and began
reading it. The more he read, the more curious he found himself
to be. It was an amalgamation of foreign words and travel ideas.
He read till it was four and night began merging into dawn. With
bags of exhaustion weighing down his eyes, the young boy made a
vow that altered the course of his destiny. He would see his father's
work published. He would let the world know the man his father
had been.

Today, Hrishikesh believed he had done his father proud.

Bound in a photograph across millions of copies, Gangaram toured new places every day. He had coffees in American Costas and German ones too. With every page he turned, he toured some more. He was the eternal traveller.

Rock 'n' Roll Redemption

He was back in his dream again. He saw himself in his bathtub, half-drowned in murky water. His breath came in deep, heaving gulps. An unknown force pressed him deeper and deeper into the water. He tried grasping the edge of the bathtub, but it slipped through his fingers, as if the tub was made of molten wax. He splashed helplessly in the water which was flooding the bathtub with every passing moment. It didn't make any sense. Where was all that water coming from? He tried to think clearly but his head throbbed with pain. He closed his eyes. When he opened them, he saw a dark figure approaching him. He narrowed his eyes, hoping to get a clear look at the face. The figure kept walking towards him and stopped right near the edge of the bathtub.

Suddenly there was blinding light everywhere. The figure was Shonali. And there was something in her hand. It was his first six-string, a Cort G200. He saw clearly the intricate flame inlays he had made on the fret boards. And the five-pointed star on the matte black body. And then suddenly Shonali flung the guitar on the floor. He cried out in pain and shock, but no sound came out of his throat. Pointed bits flew out of the guitar and hit his face. Shonali ripped the strings, wound them round his neck and began pressing the noose tighter. He choked. He couldn't breathe. 'I can't breathe Shonali, what are you doing…'

He woke up in his damp, cold bed, sweating profusely. It was unbelievable. The same dream, over and over again—and in such graphic detail. He suddenly felt very tired. He reached out to the crystal jug on the sideboard and poured himself a glass of cool water. He took a few sips. It helped clear his head a bit. He knew he couldn't sleep now. For the past one month he was having sleepless nights and these horrible recurring dreams. Exactly a month ago, Shonali had released her first solo album. It had been a big hit. She had become the toast of the town overnight. And almost overnight, his trust, his faith in love had shattered along with his dreams. He had painstakingly composed those songs over a full year, pouring his heart and soul into them, and Shonali, the conniving minx that she was, had stolen every single one of them and released them under her name.

He couldn't bear to think how it all happened, yet the memories came flooding in every night he hit the bed. The way she caressed his cheek with her long, cool fingers, the tingling sensation of her hair gently brushing his face, and the way they burst into peals of laughter at the silliest of jokes. She listened with her eyes closed, when he strummed on his guitar, as if she was enchanted by the music. She would occasionally burst into a sensuous lap dance, with nothing but the white linen bedspread around her, and then his jamming sessions would get delayed.

That reminded him of his jamming sessions. His band mates had tried their best to lift him up from his miserable state of despondency, but Shonali's betrayal had left him completely shattered. He had tried playing once, a few days after Shonali left, but his fingers had refused to flow over the strings. It was as if she hadn't just stolen his songs, but as if she had taken the life away from his fingers. For the first time in his life, he had felt absolutely terrified, unsure of whether he would be able to play again. He had taken to drinking, and whisky-tonic had become his potion, absolutely necessary for survival. He used to love cooking, but now he mostly ordered in and didn't bother to throw the pizza boxes away. His swanky, upscale apartment had become a dump. He was afraid of picking up his brand new Fender Standard Series Stratocaster, lest something terrible happened. For the past one month, he had been walking around his house like a zombie. Tonight he found himself again in the same miserable state as every night, in his cold, damp bed, sweating and shivering. He finally popped a sleeping pill and closed his tired eyes.

He woke up the next morning, absolutely drained of all his energy. He knew he had to pick himself up, dust himself and get on with his life. He desperately hoped for a sign to appear, something which would show him the way to salvation. And then he remembered his good old Cort. He had tucked it away safely in the basement, and he looked at it from time to time. It gave him inspiration when he badly needed it, it refreshed his memories when he missed his old days, and now it would give him redemption when his life was hanging from the edge of a cliff.

He climbed down to the basement and went straight to the antique cupboard that housed all his priceless gems, his memories of a lifetime—his first album jacket; his school shirt on which his classmates had scrawled parting messages; his scrapbook in which he had pasted photos of his rock idols…

And amidst all these treasures sat his baby, his Cort G200. He had bought it with money saved from the umpteen gigs of his early days. It was simple and bland when he had bought it, but he had turned it into a piece of art. The flame inlays had become a rage almost instantly, and that laid the foundation for the Shredders Custom Music Mart. He fondled the instrument lovingly, lost in the past. Those were the days. He ran his fingers over the fret boards, the strings, and felt a joyous thrill surging through him. He connected the guitar to the amplifier nearby and turned the power on. He hesitated for a microsecond, and then hit F minor. Splendid. He tuned it a little bit, and then hit G Major. Perfect! He felt as if his shackles were breaking away, and his fingers were slowly coming to life. He thought for a while and then broke into the opening chords of 'Fragile Silence'. Music boomed through the basement. His heart thumped loudly in his chest. He closed his eyes and went with the flow. His fingers switched between chords of their own accord, and the guitar felt like a part of his body. In his mind, he saw the bright lights, the stadium, the concert, and thousands of crazy fans screaming his name. He was suddenly filled with a burst of crackling energy. The fans lustily cheered his wild head banging.

He felt liberated, at ease with himself and the world. At that moment, it was just him and his guitar. As he came towards the end of the song, the cheering reached fever pitch. He finished off with a bang and threw himself at the waiting crowd. The lights started dimming and the noise died down slowly. He was back in his basement, clutching his guitar close to his body.

Tears were streaming down his face.

☙❦❧

The Love Note

TNAHSIN GARG

Another boring Sunday had rolled into my life. A day when I had almost nothing to do—not that I didn't like to sit idle, but away from office work, cuddled up in my arm chair, holding an ugly newspaper... that scenario bored me to death.

'Did you find anything?' Tara yelled from the other end of our house. Tara, my wife, had given me a daunting task of finding a second-hand sofa from the classifieds.

We had been married since two years, been together for a total of three. The year preceding our wedding was spent in dating and caressing each other. Soon we realized that we were soul mates, and should tie the knot as soon as possible. But later things didn't turn out as expected. Our married life was very much like a drunken man's lost bet. The so-called love had faded day by day since its inception. In a matter of time we had summoned a plethora of expectations from each other, but for what? Only to be left unfulfilled and discarded. Hardly a day passed when we didn't regret our hasty decision. No doubt we had our honeymoon phase with all those memories which a couple cherishes in the years to come, but still, we just never got the required amount of satisfaction we needed from this relationship. Something was still hollow, still incomplete. Now all those deep promises felt so shallow. In short, this life wasn't as romantic as it used to be or as it was supposed to be.

'Did you find it?' Tara repeated.

'Yeah… I'm still looking for it,' I grunted behind the paper. My eyes had developed a sudden interest in a glossy photograph of some young model.

Sex. A word that had become so alien to my married life. I brooded over and over.

'Stop scrutinizing bikinis, pick the classifieds from the table, and find me a good sofa,' Tara ordered, disrupting the sweet images in my mind.

Get me this, find me that. That's all I had heard from her since we tied the knot—especially since the blushing girlfriend had transformed into the frowning wife. That's primarily why I had started to hate holidays and especially Sundays, when I was saddled with endless wants and errands. Nowadays, I preferred to spend the weekends alone in my office. Not that my work was fascinating or I had an adorable secretary, it was just that I could find the rare and much sought-after peace in my cabin.

Away from my home, my family, my Tara. Tara, the girl I had loved more than anything; the girl for whom I had given up all my dreams, my career, my parents… only to abscond and live happily ever after. I hadn't imagined that 'happily ever after' would soon become 'happily never after'.

Tara came storming into the drawing room looking down at my sprawled and relaxed frame. I was still handsome, no doubt. She must have thought that as she stood still, gaping at me, unaware that I was aware of her secret glance. My broad chest, chiselled face, short hair, were once the things that really mattered to her. But now, things had changed.

There were more important matters to attend in life rather than rubbing noses.

'I'm sure you still haven't found it,' she mocked me.

'See, I don't see any in here. Maybe we look for it next Sun-'

'That's it. You don't *want* to buy it, don't you see this rickety one needs to be replaced?' her voice rose as she sat animatedly on the sofa. The sofa obeyed under her voluptuous body and squeaked in misery.

'Okay. I will look around in older papers.'

Throwing the newspaper aside in agony, I glared at her. But as I looked her over, my eyes didn't want to look elsewhere. I wanted to overlook all my rage. My eyes were filled with love but anger was pushing it away. I still didn't want to fight or spoil this Sunday morning. But it wasn't like before. I loved to be calm and amicable but she... she made it so difficult for me.

'You gonna stare at me the whole day or do some work? You have gone mad; sometimes I can't believe I married *you*.' Tara stood up pointing a finger at me.

'Are you even listening to me? My parents were right about you, you are good for nothing.' Tara shouted to the best of her voice. Reality came straggling before me. The 'good for nothing' phrase knocked my composure out at once. Last time she said this, I didn't talk to her for a whole day.

'Good for nothing? I gave away everything just to have you. I screwed my entire career to start a life with you. What good have *you* done? How you dare say *I'm* good for nothing? Damn it, it's you who does nothing all day.' Even I stood up then, shaking with anger. I don't remember the last time I had shouted so loud. I thought I loved her. Tara was shocked at first; she even cowered as I stood so fiercely. But then she wasn't going to give up.

If this was the time, let it be. Let this blasted Sunday morning decide everything.

'Don't even try to talk to me like this. I have always been a good wife.'

'Good wife? Stop it. Please. When was the last time we slept together?'

'Damn it. That's all what matters to you? When was the last time we actually went out for dinner?'

'Dinner, yeah that reminds me, when was the last time you cooked well?'

Facing each other we stood bickering like fourteen-year-olds. Did we still love each other? None of us knew the answer. The answer usually varied with our moods. For now, love ceased to exist. The talk was getting nastier with every passing second.

'You… you are just crazy, you never understand my feelings, my emotions.'

'*Your* feelings, *your* emotions, that's all what's important to you right? What about mine?'

'Yours? You actually have any? I don't think so mister! All you have in that little mind of yours are fetish desires.'

'Damn it. This talk is over,' I finished my part, waving my hands in the air.

'No, not yet. And to come to the point, all your desires are so fruitless. You can't even give me a baby.'

Silence fell everywhere. We both stopped at once. The loud debate had come to an abrupt halt. I found myself slowly settling down on the old sofa. No more words were left to be said. But the 'you-can't-even-give-me-a-baby' still kept echoing everywhere around me. Ringing in my mind, it kept burning in my heart. It was really over now. No more was needed to be said.

We had been unable to conceive a child till date; it was a hard fact. We didn't know the reason. We didn't know who was responsible because we didn't want to know. We had never cared to visit a doctor for the fear of what he or she might say. But just like the other things, the charges were pressed on me—the submissive husband. And it hurt me, it really did. A tear rolled down my left cheek. Tara saw it before I could quickly wipe it away. This moment softened her, though she tried to resist a lot. But eventually the buried love seemed to well up inside her. She too succumbed to sadness. Rivulets of tears formed on her both cheeks. But I didn't give her any chance to apologize or evoke sympathy from me. I sat motionless for a while, my face buried down in my hands. I never looked up. Perhaps I never wanted to.

An interminable lull followed.

Monday came quite slowly. Yesterday didn't want to end. We liked Mondays, for obvious reasons. By being engrossed in work we hoped to dampen the grave emotions evoked the day before. Neither of us slept properly last night. Lost in our own thoughts we lay still as if we were dead. We had thoughts which were full of regret and uncertainty.

But this Monday morning was quite different. As I woke up and got ready for office, my mind raced towards Tara. No matter how much I hated her, I still longed for her; I still loved her. I wanted to talk to her, to see her. But she was still asleep, in the other room. I didn't want to leave her either; I didn't know why it was so. Usually I left for office in the early morning hours when she was still asleep. But today it was very strange. I rather clumsily walked towards my car to leave, but then something happened. I didn't want to waste a minute then. I instantly knew what I had to do.

As I sat in the car, I thought about the little note that I had left beside her bed a few minutes ago. We used to leave such secret notes to each other when we were in college. I felt hopeful when I imagined how glad she would be at reading the note I had written:

> *Dear Tara,*
>
> *I am so sorry darling. I never wanted to hurt you. I love you so much. But I will change, for you, for us. I will go see Matt in the afternoon (he is a doctor, remember?) and see what he says. On my way back I will look for a sofa too. And be ready, tonight we will go try that new Chinese restaurant.*
>
> *I don't want anything from you; I just want you to be with me. For without you, I am so incomplete.*
>
> *I love you.*

I drove slowly on the monotonous road ahead, for I was too busy praying for a bright future. Suddenly a small piece of paper lying on the side seat caught my gaze. I instantly picked it up and read slowly. It was Tara's beautiful curved handwriting. The note read:

> *Dear Rahul,*
>
> *I know yesterday was a very hard day for us. I feel so guilty, it's my fault, you loved me so much but I always demanded more. I'm sorry. I am so careless sometimes, but I have always... loved you.*

Tonight when you come, you will find a changed Tara, a devoted and loving wife. Embracing you in my arms I will hold you the whole night. Don't come late, I will cook for you a hot plate of pasta (your favourite!).

I really don't need that blasted sofa anymore, nor do I need a child. I just need you. Yes, Rahul, I need you. Without you, I am so hollow.

I love you.

I couldn't help smiling. I actually stopped the car and laughed with joy for over a minute. I spent the rest of the day re-reading that lovely note countless times.

Shimmer

LIPI MEHTA

Lalita was seven years old when she started wearing glasses. To tease her mother, she would often remove them and speak of what she saw. Shapes of people and objects would all reduce to colour right in front of her eyes. She never knew how to explain this to her mother and so, she would simply say, 'I can't see anything.' Her mother would coax her to wear her glasses again and just like that, the world would be full of outlines again—the ones that she could draw and the ones that she could trace. 'It's only because you read in dim light,' her mother would say, pointing to her glasses. This was true; Lalita often read in torchlight, being careful not to wake her mother up. However, it was her mother who had first introduced her to storytelling. Some of the first stories that Lalita had heard were from her. And each night, through the books she read, various characters would come to life under the folds of her blanket. As years passed, she was grateful that this relationship she shared with books remained immutable.

On the day her mother bought her a diary, Lalita realized that it was probably time to turn her imagination into writing. She sought help from some of her favourite authors and tried to imitate them at first. Failing consistently, she started scribbling notes—a few observations from here and there. Her diary became a jumble of thoughts, a game of Scrabble where bits and pieces could be joined to derive meaning. Lalita always saw her as a writer from within and could not accept the fact that maybe, her mother, though gifted with the power of storytelling, had not bequeathed her with the same. She would thus resort to reading again and force herself to sleep. As time passed, she saw herself receding into a world where her writing was for her eyes only. Everyone knew that she loved reading but hardly anyone had ventured into the depths of her closet where her diaries lay, waiting to be opened and read.

When Lalita left her hometown to study literature at college, she met many others who shared her likes and dislikes. In these new friendships, she found people who loved their coffee as much as their wine and company as much as their solitude. During one class, her teacher spoke about the existence of a parallel world that books often give rise to. The class spoke about how it was easy for the reader to let go of his surroundings for a point in time while being absolutely still. At night, Lalita thought about this. She wanted to sleep but she wondered why books compelled her to keep reading even when these were stories that would never be seen in the real world. Later, her friend would sum the reason up in one simple line, 'Only when you believe in fantasy do you enjoy it.'

As college neared its end, Lalita reminisced about the three years that she had spent in this unknown city. The city had welcomed her with open arms and she felt dejected now at leaving its warm embrace. She was going back home to her mother who had not been keeping well lately. As she reached home, she saw how everything in her room lay still—as still as she had left it. In one corner of her room lay an old trunk in which she had put most of her books before leaving for college. Today, it seemed almost like a trousseau which she would take with her wherever she would go next. In the trunk, she found an old diary of hers which was half-filled. She flipped through it and stared at the empty pages for a while.

Her mother's voice had softened and so had the creases on her forehead. She seemed more relaxed, more composed. Constant bouts of fever had weakened her and she had stopped teaching at the university as well. After three years of being away from home, Lalita saw herself as someone who could change herself according to her surroundings. She started taking care of her mother and quickly got accustomed to this sense of responsibility that she now lived with. One night, she sat alone in her room and went through her books and old diaries. Caked with dust, they lay motionless, prompting her to touch them, to re-read all that she had once read and written. As she read some of her old writing, she realized that it was buoyant—it was not too heavily-worded and she had given her words space to breathe in. In this writing, Lalita saw in herself a passion that she hadn't seen before, for this was the passion of words which she had been seeking her entire life. She realized that being away from home had given her a different perspective altogether. With one of her diaries in her hand, she walked towards her mother's room. Her mother welcomed her with a smile and beckoned her to sit next to her. That night, Lalita read one of her stories to her mother. She saw her story as a lullaby, cradling her mother to sleep.

Almost every night after that, she read a little bit to her mother. It was a humbling feeling for her as her storyteller assumed the role of a listener each night. This role reversal imbued Lalita with a sense of confidence—she felt even happier when her mother demanded a story from her. She felt closer to her mother—their relationship had been strengthened by this string of stories. She tried writing a little each day and was not as saddened by failure as she had been before. A few years ago, she had seen herself as just company to her mother; today, she was her companion. Lalita took her books out of her trunk and arranged them in her old bookshelf. Instead of feeling saddened at not being able to write like her favourite writers, she now saw their books as something that had shaped her thinking.

That night, she narrated an idea she had for a story to her mother. Her mother caressed her hands, smiled at her and said, 'Start now.' In these two words, Lalita found many words which she had been looking for. She realized that her mother had indeed given her the gift of storytelling but she had done it silently, gracefully. Lalita picked up a pen and walked inside her room. She seemed even more resolute as she carefully removed a diary from the bookshelf in her room. She opened it to the smell of her mother's hands as specks of dust flew out of the pages. She coughed a little but as she looked at them dancing around her, all she could see was but, a burst of shimmer in the air.

The Pillow Knows Our Secrets

HINA SIDDIQUI

The greatest playground of humanity is the chamber where you make love.

The first time he turned away from her after, she let it pass. Her heart contracted a little, her smile wavered momentarily, her skin prickled with goose bumps and she displayed inexplicable hostility by throwing a pillow into the wall when he wasn't looking. However, she chose to ignore it and they made banal talk for a few minutes, following which sleep claimed him, and eventually her. Oddly however, the more often it happened, and it happened without fail every time they slept together, instead of her growing more accustomed to his vagaries, each time grated her heart a little harder than the last.

They had been together, in every sense of the word, for three months now. She was an architect and he worked in marketing. His parents lived in a town in another state and she was old enough and established enough for her parents to make daring stabs at liberality. They had been friends ever since he did some marketing work for her firm and it didn't take long for amour to barge its way in to their frequent meetings and dalliances. He was smart, decisive and ambitious. She was demure, pensive and fond of reading fantasy novels. They complemented each other well and their relationship won quickly, the approval of friends on both sides of the fence. They watched movies together, had short work-day lunches and long talks on the mobile after dinner. He made her laugh, she made him happy and it was what it was—the beginning of a wonderfully average romance.

The decision to take it to the next level was made convenient one winter day. Tempers had been flying at her firm, with her in the eye of the storm, owing mainly to several unmet deadlines and a severely strained budget. She had to work late and that meant cancelling the long-awaited dinner date with him. He sounded colder than the evening air on the phone and his presumed lack of understanding drove her up the wall. She railed and ranted, mostly in her head, then made the grievous error of sending not a few texts, full of self-pitying accusations and gnarly end-of-the-world sentiments. Although it is easy for love gurus to preach abstinence from expectation, expectations unwittingly become the cornerstones of most relationships in our transactional world. He *must* pay for the date... she *must* not interfere with his friends... he *must* be nice when she's PMSing... she *must*... well you get the picture. No one, sensibly enough, discusses these things openly before getting into a relationship and for the most part, they do not matter. Unless of course, one of the partners fail in this unspoken commitment. Then the edifice of love and mutual trust threatens to fall apart under the strain of equalling scores and one-upmanship.

The point is, her career was important and as such, by failing to respond amiably to her standing him up, he had in effect failed her and thus, at least in her head, deserved the ill-worded tirade that criticized everything from his ability to love to his inability to keep the dishes in the sink after a meal.

She worked furiously past midnight, channelling much of her anger in to complicated diagrams of spaces for the client. Her resentment was however, by no means spent, and she fully intended to continue the fight the next day, as soon as she was brushed and flossed. It flabbergasted her beyond imagination then, when she walked out of her nearly deserted office building, with its lecherous night watchman, to find him waiting for her, shivering on his bike.

'Didn't want you to catch a cab this late,' he mumbled as he kicked off, literally charming the pants off of her with his possessiveness.

He took her to his place of course, where pizza and thoughtful pints of beer awaited and by the time he was done placing the plates in the sink, she was ready to explode with sensual excitement. She had had men before, but he was the first she attempted warming the bed with, and though inexperienced, she was willing. And he… well, let's just say she had never ripped a pillow apart with her bare hands ever before.

And then when her body was pleasurably aching, her mind spinning and the commode threatening to be clogged by used condoms, he had turned away.

Now most people believe that women have this unnecessary longing for the post-coital cuddle. For a woman it completes the act, for a man, it probably means having a numb arm in the morning after a night spent pillowing a sleeping head. It is hard to say what is the norm and what is negotiable in the bedroom, but feeling alone after the most celebrated act of coming together is probably not the best way to end the night. But she was determined not to be stereotypical. There's enough whining about sex in American soap operas and lifestyle magazines and as a woman of today, she became determined to invest herself in the activity and reap the maximum pleasure. So there were weeks were she furtively Googled positions at work, wore expensive perfumes, acquired a taste for Victoria's Secret and basically tried every intelligent girl's tool to becoming the hottest thing to hit the bed. How many times in a night, how many nights in a week—it became her manna and her labour, his desire and her propensity for arousing it, a yardstick for her vitality. And by her own measure, she was as vital as they got.

But still, the doubt remained.

Initially, he made his excuses–

'Have to use the bathroom.'

'Need a smoke.'

'Just going to fix us a drink.

'Have an important email to send.'

'Uff, its hot… need to turn on the fan.'

But of late, all he did was finish and turn away and she ended up caressing the pillow instead. She wasn't dissatisfied, not by a long shot. Their life together was as adorable as ever. And he was a gentleman in bed, the kind who was also a secret agent and just what Her Majesty ordered. But even multiple orgasms began to lose their appeal in the face of that simple end-rejection.

Six more months went by. The wound began to fester and perhaps she could have used communication as the balm. Friends told her as much and remarkably, it did occur to her that it was impossible for him to know what she wanted unless she told him. He had after all, exhibited none of the finer traits of mind-reading. But it was a conversation for which she could conceive no beginning. How do you tell someone that all the delightful things they do for you—the surprise weekend getaways, the being nice to your parents, the statuses on Facebook—are fogged indistinct by their unwillingness to hold you when you need it?

And it is exactly questions of this sort that shouldn't be going round and round and round in your head when you are pulling out into rush hour traffic on any given Monday. To say she never saw the car coming would be an understatement. Although, to be fair, whoever considers the possibility that a perfectly sane driver, moving his car under the speed limit in the right lane would run them over? She was helped to her swaying feet by half a dozen strangers who, very well-meaningly, told her, she was lucky to be alive and that, forget driving, she probably shouldn't touch a steering wheel with a ten foot long pole. Little did they know their admonishments were in vain because there are few things in heaven and on earth that can cause as many calamities as a girl in love.

On the gurney in the emergency room, she tried to fixate over an irrelevant point in space to blunt the pain of the stitches and found her mind involuntarily drifting to him. She imagined him holding her hand, squeezing it, wincing just slightly as the needle made its excruciating way, five times, to her head, his hand caressing her hair as the nurse slathered tincture all over her bruises in the most inhumane way possible. She watched in her mind's colour, his brow knitting in anger as the doctor scoffed at a 'woman's road sense' and felt, very sincerely, his arms closing around her protectively as the needle came closer to her skin than he would permit any sharp thing to come. And if she left the clinic, bamboozling the doctors with her inane smile, well, who could blame the poor, moonstruck child?

She sat in her room later, cuddling a pillow, being pampered silly by her parents who, like many of their generation, believed that scalding hot chicken soup and overreacting were the solution to all problems. Well, at least they cared, her parents. As for him, she didn't tell him about the accident, but a mutual friend who had to be informed so she could cover for her at work, let the cat very much out of the bag. He called her then.

'Why do I have to find out that you have had an accident through someone else?'

That was the first thing he said to her.

He never asked her if she was wounded, or if she needed anything or even if she was okay. In the middle of his asserting the alleged authority of boyfriends, the shots of painkillers the nurse had rammed into her just this morning seemed to stop working and so she hung up. But cutting the line didn't mean she could sever his voice. She remembered how for the longest time, sometimes in a joke, sometimes when they fought, especially when she tried to bring up her intimacy issues, his reason for everything was that she couldn't see the larger picture. He never explained what he meant by that and she found herself feeling too puzzlingly insecure by the comment to question him about it. And today she felt more than ever that she couldn't see it—the larger picture—and perhaps getting her nearly killed was the Universe's way of gently reminding her to get some goddamn perspective.

And just in time too... for he came to see her in the evening, after work, carrying an electrifyingly yellow bunch of gerberas.

Maybe it had something to do with the fact that her heart couldn't stand any more dejection, or that she had needed help to visit the bathroom seven times today or maybe that she had a few days of paid leave from work to regret her actions in, but as soon as her parents, enthusiastic as ever, left the immature girl and her super-loving boyfriend alone...

'Will you marry me?' she blurted out.

And here he was expecting to hug her, hear the story of the misadventure and get home before the big game started.

'Are you alright?' he ventured as a comeback.

Too late for that now.

'I'm alive and I'd like an answer.'

Silence... also didn't work.

Staring intensely with five stitches over the brow... worked.

'I don't think I'm ready,' he said.

A fair enough answer, if only he hadn't been palpitating like a llama in heat.

'Soooo... when will you be ready?'

Waiting a little longer.

'I can see your jaw moving a lot, but there are no words coming out of your mouth.'

What followed were a series of audible clicks, hmms and coughs, that were either a new language or just what a man would do if, say, his girlfriend beat him in an arm-wrestling spat on the second date, while his buddies from school were watching with beers in hand. After a few minutes, even the neighbour's dog would have guessed that what it had sipped at the toilet had been their relationship going down.

The end is always abrupt when you're not expecting it.

He left, ears red and head confused, never to return to the girl he had slept with for nine months. And she lay there, injured and hurt, watching the man she loved and needed turn away for the last time. Then she turned to her pillow and cried.

☙

The Cab Driver

JANICE RODRIGUES

Gopal Varma squirmed against the blazing afternoon heat that seemed to fill every nook and cranny of his ancient cab. He had been spending his afternoon naps there for the past two years—each hotter than the last—but this year seemed downright unbearable. As he swatted away yet another mosquito, he cursed the scorching sun and his sweltering, heat-absorbing cab. *I'd probably get more sleep in an oven*, he mused. Too hot to get sleep, and yet too lazy to actually wake up, Gopal hovered in between, his eyes shut tight, his arm carefully positioned over his face to keep the sun away... which is why it took only a light tapping on his window to stir him from sleep. As Gopal opened one bleary eye, he found himself looking at a heavyset man, with dark skin and a bold moustache, staring down at him.

'Brother!' the man's voice was powerful, loud. 'I need a good person to take my friend to Borivali. Will you take the job?'

That immediately caught Gopal's attention. 'Borivali, you say?' he mused. They were at Churchgate right now; a journey to Borivali would easily earn him around 500 rupees. And God knew, he needed the money.

'I'll do it brother,' he called out, 'Where is this friend of yours?'

'Wait right here, she'll be out of this building in ten minutes,' the man nodded towards the old, derelict building across the street from where Gopal was parked. Gopal nodded sleepily, managed to raise himself into a sitting position and started to button on his khaki-coloured shirt. *Damn this heat*, he found himself thinking again, *makes everyone so drowsy*. As he sat waiting for the lady he started to wonder what he would do with the extra 500 rupees. Save up for his rent, or send it to his family back home in the village. Or even better, he could treat himself to a nice meal. It had been long since he had eaten in a restaurant.

When the woman finally arrived, Gopal felt a twinge of shock. She was definitely not like anyone he expected—a plain housewife or mistress of the heavyset man who had called him. Instead he found himself staring at a slim, fair girl no older than twenty-five. Quite good looking, the lady walked like a princess, one hand daintily clutching her branded purse, the other, a pink Dell laptop bag. Behind her, the security guard carried a larger pink suitcase which he pushed into the trunk of the taxi.

The woman sat at the back without saying a word other than ordering him to take her to Borivali. She then pulled on her sunglasses, kicked off her expensive-looking heels and put on her earphones. Gopal felt a rush of hatred as he watched this delicate princess covered in designer brands. How was the world fair when people like him slaved all day and still didn't earn as much as this spoiled little girl would be earning on her first job? Courtesy of a fancy degree from a private college paid for with daddy's money.

He had just crossed the JJ Flyover and it was only then that he noticed he was speeding. *I guess my mind's just not into driving today*, he thought glumly. Instead he stared irritably at the girl through the rear-view mirror. She had perfectly straight hair, no doubt an expensive do at the parlour. Her face was hidden behind layers of make-up. He felt that anger rising again. His own daughter would consider herself lucky if she could one day work in a beauty parlour!

They were crossing the prestigious Phoenix Mall when suddenly the woman signalled him to stop. He pulled over right in front of the mall, confused. Had he not understood the destination correctly?

'You wait here,' the woman ordered, 'Keep all my things safe.' She spoke in a heavily accented voice. She then picked up her branded handbag, put on the heels she could barely walk in and trod delicately from the cab. Gopal stared at her in shock and surprise and as she pranced into the mall, without a second thought for her luggage or her laptop.

It didn't take him more than two minutes to find his eyes trailing over the laptop. Expensive or not, it could probably pay for his rent for the next six months! And who knew what else was there in the other suitcase. Branded clothes are also worth a lot second-hand. And they could easily be sold.

He didn't know how long he stared at the suitcase, just thinking. He could be in trouble with the law, but the girl didn't seem too bright. He doubted whether she had even glanced at his license plate. And what was all this stuff to her anyway? If he were to take it and go what was the worse that would happen? Daddy would buy her another expensive laptop. On the other hand, a little extra money meant the world to him. He was the one with a family to support.

Once he had made his decision, Gopal acted swiftly, reversing the cab and driving out of the mall's parking lot. He could feel his heart beating faster than ever, and he even imagined the girl yelling—running after him, calling the police. But nothing happened. He successfully drove off and joined the main road.

As the mall slowly disappeared behind him, Gopal felt his pulse return to normal. All that fear was now replaced with a new energy, a new excitement. He made sure he had driven far enough from the mall in the next half an hour before stopping in front of a rundown building. As he parked the car carefully, he felt his excitement grow. He first checked the laptop bag—the pink laptop looked almost brand new. He had never seen anything so beautiful in his life.

He walked slowly and opened the trunk with excitement. In this beautiful moment it actually felt like the pink suitcase there was calling out to him. No, indeed it was actually humming. It took him only a second to register. He pulled the zip open to find a strange metal device. On the front, in electric red numbers, was a countdown. With dread, he gazed at the number. As he stared transfixed at the numbers, he realized what a fool he had been. How the girl was nothing he had thought her to be. How she had played him, effortlessly. Two seconds left.

And then the bomb went off.

The next day every newspaper carried a headline about the Mumbai terrorist attacks. Three bomb blasts, all in South Mumbai, all having taken place in taxis. The three taxi drivers had died on the spot, but strangely there seemed to be no passengers in any of the cabs. The bombs had left craters on the side of the road, and as a result, different routes had to be closed. The people of Mumbai read the articles, shook their heads in exasperation and forgot about it as soon as they threw away the paper. In their minds, it didn't really matter. Mumbai would survive. It always did.

᠁

Our Friend Junaid

ANIKET DASGUPTA

Naina's Note

Junaid and I met in college; he wanted to become a film-maker and I wanted to become an author. He wasn't the world's greatest boyfriend but he was nice. He wasn't really all that social; he would just smile awkwardly when anyone said anything to him. We had great fun initially getting to know each other. But it started getting complicated towards the end. We dated for over a year until Junaid wanted to break up. Not that I didn't want to, but he wanted it more than me. I had begun to become bitter by the end of it; we fought, the fights got physical. And to add to that, Junaid became so very obsessive. Besides, I didn't really like the fact that he smoked marijuana. I knew it had to end. And it did. In a few months he became a completely different person—someone I didn't identify with any longer. I realized, he had been like that all along. I gave up so much for him, but he was self-centred and so full of himself. It was just that I didn't see it that way. I had started thinking like him; he had gotten under my skin. I loved him, but I had to move on eventually. I started seeing Sid. I don't think Junaid took it too well.

He started avoiding me in college and I really didn't care to know about what he did or where he went after college. He kept in touch with only a few people, Rajdip being one of them. Rajdip did tell me a bit about him going away to some place up in the north, where he was living with a few Israeli hippies.

I read about him on a blog a year ago, where he was advocating the legalization of marijuana through his film. That was so typically him, he would stand up for what he thought was right, no matter how wrong it was. He looked very different in the photo in that article, nothing like the way he looked in college.

I wouldn't say that I saw signs of this when I was with him but his sudden bouts of ranting about how everything is so meaningless did scare me back then. Albeit being very whimsical, the guy was good at heart.

I wish I could tell him that I did care for him; I just couldn't show it after we broke up. I wish I could tell him that everything he did and said affected me. But none of it makes any difference now.

I couldn't believe what I heard, it was so sudden. I'll really miss him.

Sid's Note

He was my best friend. I always thought that someday things between us would be fine again. I did not see this coming. Junaid was what one would call unconventional. He was unpredictable. Everything he did was unexpected.

My fondest memory of Junaid is of the time he was over at my family's coffee plantation in Coorg. He didn't want to go home because according to him he did not have one. He told me of his deepest fears, his love for the unknown and unchartered, and his dreams of seeing his vision on screen. He would light his joint and change the way we see things. He would seem happy all the time, but I knew there were layers of him that nobody knew about.

This was a different Junaid—not the recluse he'd later turn into. This Junaid was an eloquent dreamer. This was also the time he decided it was best that he ended things with Naina, despite being hopelessly in love with her. He had these commitment issues you see, he wasn't sure if this is what he wanted.

He did end things with her when we went back to college. When I realized I liked Naina, I didn't know how I'd tell him. But I did.

Junaid smiled as if nothing happened and he said, 'I am happy for you Sid, I am glad you guys found each other.'

That was the last time he spoke to me properly. I hated what he was turning into. He was negative about everything that surrounded him, including Naina. He stopped hanging out with all of us; he'd randomly disappear for days at hand. Something happened after that. He distanced himself from almost everybody who used to be close to him. I just wish I could go back in time and forget everything and just push him back to being who he was. But then I'd stop him from being him.

He got some money out of a few videos he made for others. He used to save most of it, I really don't know why. Everyone thought he'd become one of those people who have potential but don't succeed in doing much. Everyone had criticized his work as indulgent and unusual. The films he made in college were also filled with self-loathing; a lot of them didn't even make sense.

He always wanted to travel; he wasn't the type that would work in an office. I don't think he wanted a job. While the rest of us were out there going mad over placements, Junaid would sit in his room and write.

As I said before, I didn't see this coming. Junaid was meant for something great. I tried getting through to him many times prior to all of this. His girlfriend Mia wouldn't let me talk to him saying he didn't want to. I really don't know if she was lying or if she wasn't. I just wish she was. Somewhere deep down, I think I am partly responsible for this. I wasn't around him when he needed me the most. That's something I'll regret all my life. I wish I was just there for him.

Mia's Note

I met Junaid in Dharamshala. I had just returned from my military conscription back home and had been living in Dharamshala for about two months. Junaid was working as a volunteer video editor at a pro-independence Tibetan media outfit. It was voluntary work but they took care of his stay and food. He would also work freelance and make some money to live the way he did. I met him at a coffee shop in McLeod Ganj. He was holed up in one corner working on his laptop. He didn't seem like the other Indian tourists there. He looked harmless enough for me to begin talking to him. A lot of coffee-powered conversations followed that. Junaid did not have a phone, he said he had lost it and didn't need one. It worked fine because McLeod Ganj is a small place, and there weren't too many places he'd go to.

He said he loved my perspective. Initially, he seemed like all of them young pseudo-artistic drifters. But as I got to know him better, I realized there was more to him than just that. His thoughts had depth. And he would go on to any extent to nourish them. The strange bit about him was that he was very scared of relationships. This was strange because he was such a free soul. He wanted to make a film about things that he cared, that's where the idea for *Freedom* germinated I guess. There was a dark side to him. I am pretty sure he would have been a little more bearable had he not been such a cynic. However, he was different while he was around others and when he was alone. He was vulnerable in his solitude and the exact opposite otherwise. I guess that's what he wanted. He didn't care much for others, except a few people who somehow mattered to him. And yet he wouldn't want to talk to any of his older friends. Sid got my number from Rajdip and tried getting in touch with him. He refused to talk.

He was a passionate lover and maybe that's why the women liked him around. He would often joke that he knew how he would die—AIDS or a really expensive paternity lawsuit. He fucked around with others even when we started 'dating' and I didn't stop him.

When you stop someone from doing something they really want to, you are just making them hide it even more from you.

And knowing Junaid, it wasn't anything more than sex for him. He was too complicated to allow another person into his complications. He had a fetish for the colours red and yellow; they were his black and white.

He had a fascination for obscure books and conspiracy theories. I don't think he believed in them but I think he wanted to. He would never talk about his childhood or college life, because he thought they weren't worth talking about in retrospect. He also painted a very pretty picture of how things were between him, Sid and Naina but having read his diary, I know things weren't the way he claimed they were. I guess that's when he stopped trusting people so easily.

People keep saying that he was a stoner, but he was what he was. I mean alcohol kills more people than marijuana can ever kill, yet it is socially wrong to consume it. When Junaid finally started working on *Freedom* and started campaigning for marijuana legalization through it, a lot of people told him that this was against the act of nature including his stupid dealer Danny, because this would put rules on a business that is otherwise, largely lawless.

I last saw him the day before he was to go to Delhi for some work regarding the distribution of his film. He was so content and happy. That's the happiest I ever saw him. He told me how he wanted to trek to Triund with me on his return.

I am yet to come to terms with what has happened; I just wish this were a bad dream.

Danny's Note

Juno was like my brother from another mother. He started me off. I was just a small-time dealer back in college. He hooked me up with some really good stuff and people who wanted it. I asked him why he wasn't doing it himself. He said something about not being good at business or something... no I think it was because he didn't know how Naina would react to it... maybe it was both of those reasons. Whatever, he started me off. And he was around for me whenever I needed him to be. He didn't trust people easily; there were only a handful he really trusted. He trusted Naina more than he loved her, he was scared of relationships. He trusted Sid too, but then circumstances fucked him up all the more. His fear of relationships turned into hatred. He distanced himself from everything that he identified himself with. He would spend hours in my house smoking up. I started getting worried; I told him that I'd stop selling to him. He said it was momentary and it would lapse. It did lapse. Most folks don't know what happened to him after finished college. He grew disillusioned with his life and decided to travel away from all of this madness. He went to McleodGanj in Dharamshala. He was familiar with the place; both of us had gone there for our internships. He decided to stay there and did a few odd video jobs to keep things going. This is when everyone else decided to run the never-ending rat race. How many people would be able to do that?

He did have a thing for that Mia chick he met in Dharamshala but he was always scared of being in relationships after Naina. He wouldn't want to make the same mistakes again.

Then he got involved in that stupid legalization shit. I had gone to meet him at McLeod Ganj. He told me about his film. He didn't see the stupidity of the whole thing. This was India; people don't really like talking about weed that way. It's all behind closed doors, a lot like how we don't discuss sex and sexuality openly. He stopped speaking to me when I told him to get out of all of this. Yeah, I had my own reasons. I mean, I am a pot dealer at the end of the day.

I won't lie; I knew this would happen some day or the other. I just didn't know it would happen this way. Let's hope he's happy wherever he is.

Rajdip's Note

Junaid Mikhail Ali was my client, but more importantly, he was a friend. As his lawyer, I must admit he was a rather daunting client. As a friend, he was irreplaceable. Most people didn't know the truth about Junaid's life. That is because he wanted it that way and I shall respect his wishes and adhere to the same. He told me of his idea for *Freedom* before it became such a big deal. If you do watch the film, you will realize that marijuana was just one bit of the film. It was about a man finding himself and living free. Marijuana legalization was just one of the things the movie advocated, because the movie was Junaid's life and he himself advocated the legalization of marijuana.

I spoke to Junaid about a month ago, he had just returned

from a film festival in Canada. He was telling me how people loved *Freedom*. He also told me how he had some legality to discuss because he intended to sell and distribute his film. I met him and we discussed the options he had for the same. That was the last time I met him.

He was shot dead by a member of the drug nexus in New Delhi; he had gone to the city to sell the rights of his film to a Dutch documentary distribution company. He had signed that contract before his death. Now that he is gone, the royalty from *Freedom* is to be used to continue his fight for marijuana legalization.

He had no family after his parents died when he was ten; he had grown up in an orphanage. He did have some money, all of which he has left to be distributed equally amongst Mia Cohen, Daniel Mistry, Naina Sharma, Siddharth Cariappa and myself.

I have nothing else to say, I just hope he found his peace; this world wasn't good enough for him.

Setting Sun

NAMAN SARAIYA

One rainy morning, groggy-eyed but (only) determined to finish the assignment, I woke up with a start, owing to that damn phone call. What the fuck was I doing asleep, I thought, with the laptop still on my stomach, before finally answering the call.

'Dude, class got canned for today.'

'No way. I stayed up the whole night to finish this presentation. This is not happening. Bro, if you're kidding, I'll lead the war to your impotency.'

'Calm down and go to fucking sleep.'

I couldn't take anymore of Bob Dylan telling me that the times are indeed changing, while superheroes punch each other in the face, against the backdrop of World War II. All of this while, I take a simple comic and make it the victim of some strange analysis which is supposed to score me an A+ because, apparently, that matters. If I may add so, it matters only to your relatives at social gatherings, because there's no other way to scale you better in their phoney, closed mindset. Clearly, I was pissed off at that, besides another gem of our education system—group assignments. I mean, what's the point of them? Trying to get different people together in such an odd way and hope they find a way to work together and other such rubbish.

'Hi, class got cancelled. I'm not lying, before you doubt me.'

'Oh God. Okay, at least I get to sleep.'

'Do you want to hang out today, or maybe go somewhere?'

'Like, where?'

'We can decide later. I'll call the others. You just show up, once you're awake.'

'Cool.'

'Sleep well.'

But I'm still partially annoyed by the way events had transpired over the last few hours or so. I didn't want to smoke another cigarette or undertake the third cup of coffee at the hour when most others around the country are prepped for work. I lived with a colleague-turned-friend of mine. I only worked part time now, having enrolled myself for a course in photojournalism a couple of months ago. It's a good time to relax and reflect upon life, having worked for a bit—but I guess I was way too young for it. I enjoyed it nonetheless, toying around with new equipment that I'd get my hands on from friends and fellow enthusiasts.

'Hi. Are you up?'

'Somewhat. Are you heading here?'

'Should be there in twenty. At Bombay Central on a fast.'

'Super.'

The mad scramble began once I saw the words Bombay Central. That meant another six minutes to Dadar, then another four to Bandra and fifteen minutes to get to my apartment that was in a ridiculous mess. Thirty minutes to a potential first date, and I was lying in bed, debating with myself about the pros and cons of being single. Once the doorbell rang, all these ideas would flutter away into the horizon and everything she would say would seem interesting. After preparing a mental checklist, I began ticking off things one by one—clean room, make bed, bathe and check for coffee and milk.

Here's a little back story to the entire scrambling and second and third set of text messages—it's this girl in my class. I must confess that I have a terrible weakness, an almost fatal antagonist towards my romantic life—curly hair. This case was no different and within weeks of meeting her, I knew I had begun warming up to the idea of dating again. It had almost become a pattern of sorts, where I fell into the same pit of failed stints, over and over again—and every attempt performed the duty of resurrecting my faith in relationships altogether. However, this time, I had given myself a fairly adequate thinking period to make the call about whether I really wanted to date again.

A friend of mine, significantly older than I was, often told me how I behaved like an old man at most given points in time. It never occurred to me per se, but when he insisted on the same thing a few times over, I saw some light in the matter. My mother was right—I had been in way too many relationships for my age. For me, I often cited it as an anecdote illustrating why relationships could be either the most amazing or the most terrible thing to happen to someone. Almost like a cycle, I was falling into the same pit and this time, it felt strangely familiar but also better. Maybe it was just a consolation I churned up in my head about how I was beginning to feel about life and my social presence without a girlfriend for over a year. When was the last time that had happened? Never, since the time I had discovered the concept of dating when in the tenth grade. *Good call*, said the voice inside my head.

I warned myself about not running into awkward scenarios, as a result of doing something stupid that could possibly ruin another social situation. And I didn't want any of that happening in a classroom that is just thirty people, most of whom I had never spoken to. I wasn't being a snob really, but just weary of what was happening around me all the time—thinking over life-kind-of things and focusing my energies on actually learning—except of course till that one day. This girl I keep mentioning walked in with her hair freshly shampooed and open—curly in all its glory, sending me into an uncertain, miraculously long daze.

When I did speak to her though, every single time after that and until this day, I'll confess to this one thing—I tried really hard not to appear head-over-heels and almost foolish about my interest in her, all but for three reasons. To begin with, she had *Death Cab for Cutie* on her iPod, which made it a green signal and moving on to the next, her curly hair. I cannot mention enough times, how important a part curls play in these ridiculous games men and women play with each other. And well, finally, she was cute, and interesting. This was all seeming too analytical all of a sudden and I tried to reason why this was happening right now. Surely it wasn't that suspicious cigarette on the table, which I smoked a few minutes ago. It couldn't have been because there wasn't one in the first place.

And in this extremely intense, philosophical moment of thought there is nothing worse than the sound of the doorbell ringing and knowing that you miscalculated someone's arrival. The checklist had been taken care of, but maybe something was off? No, there wasn't, but I was just procrastinating.

'Hi.' (Of a kind that extended into more than a few seconds.)

'What's up?'

This is the 'awkward hug moment', because you're not sure how to go about it—is it more casual and friendly because you're home and not on campus or will it come off as creepy? Or should it just be a side hug and left that way, for safety measures I guess. It's one of the most interesting things when you really think about it—because it's often an indicator of how things will shape eventually between two people getting acquainted with each other at a given point in time. I don't know if I'm being over categorical or just unnecessarily stupid, but I guess it is justified having finally opened up to the idea of dating someone, and not being awkward about any sort of commitment to anyone. I think we shared a regular hug, and phew, was I happy.

'Could I have some coffee?'

'Sure. With milk?'

'No.'

'And sugar?'

'I'll manage that.'

'So, what took you so long?'

'The damn traffic, which never lets me down. Always ruining my mood.'

'Relax.'

'Yeah, I'm fine.'

'Don't seem to be.'

'Okay, sorry. Now tell me, why did you want to meet?'

'What?'

'Are you sure you don't want to say anything?'

'No, why'd you think so?'

'Never mind.'

'Want to watch a movie?'

'Shouldn't we wait for the others to get here?'

'Err, I guess. Don't think they're getting here before an hour or so.'

'Are you really sure you don't want to say something to me? Because you're really being strange right now.'

How? How was I being strange? I took every step to be careful about not giving away any signs and here she was presuming something was wrong with me and that I had something to say. Sure, I did, but I wasn't entirely sure about how I'd be able to get myself to say it. There was also the immense risk of coming across as a weird douche-like character from an American teen movie, both of which were things I'd rather not associate myself with. Back to the conversation then—I convinced her that I hadn't got anything to say to her and also added a convenient 'not yet' after the last time she asked me the question. This was while the movie was still on, and she was holding my hand—and I saw her turn the other way and smile a wry smile.

It seemed like a terrible day in the morning with rains and cancelled classes, but it gradually got better in the afternoon with the sun showing up, forced preparedness, awkward moments and finally the movie with some coffee—all thanks to this one girl. Not a bad day after all, I thought to myself as I sat beside her in the balcony. There was an odd, but comforting silence that lingered on for most of the evening, as the sun set and the sky, blended more hues into its palette. She suddenly turned towards me, still holding her cup of coffee that she had reheated about three times now, because she kept forgetting to drink it while the movie was on. I wasn't sure of how to react, but I think she turned because some lyrics from a song that was playing in the drawing room wafted in. Maybe she was trying to prove a point.

His head was a city / of paper buildings / and the echoes that remained. / Of old friends and lovers / their features bleeding, / together, in his brain.

And in this moment, nothing seemed more right or wrong including all the over procrastination from the days before. There she was sitting beside me, in my balcony holding a cup of coffee, looking into my eyes as the lyrics painted an image of me in her head—almost as if she was saying all of this to me, and my faith in the concept of dating coming alive at the same time—with the sun setting and its warmth beginning to feel all-encompassing. Surely this wasn't a scene from a Wes Anderson movie?

'Are you scared?'

'A bit.'

'Of what?'

'Girls who want to date after kissing you once.'

'Funny. Are there many like them?'

'I seem to have bumped into quite a few of them.'

'You? What are you scared of?'

'Intimacy.'

'You're practically in my face right now. I don't think you're scared.'

'Because it's you.'

'Oh really? Flattering.'

'How cocky.'

'Always.'

'But can I ask you one thing?'

'Sure. Though, can it wait?'

'For what?

'Either I'm going to have to kiss you now, to avoid any strangeness or you can go ahead and ask me what you had to.'

'What?'

'I've been resting my forehead against yours for the last three minutes.'

'Oh, right.'

'So?'

'So.'

After what seemed like an eternity, I found both of us sitting in the same place as we were while talking, forehead against the other. Of course, the sun had entirely set—and I had also decided to let the sun of my procrastination set with the day. Maybe the colours were just about beautiful during that sunset, which these film guys often called the magic hour. No one ever warned us about the darkness that would follow shortly, disregarding all the beauty that spread over the skies just minutes ago. But she looked into the cup of coffee, with her head down almost inviting me to kiss her again.

I lifted her head, using her chin and rested my forehead against her's, for the second time in under fifteen minutes and she didn't flinch.

'I thought you wanted to ask me something?'

'I did.'

'Go on.'

'This way?'

'Why not? Weren't you going to do it earlier anyway?'

'True, but…'

'It's comfortable.'

'Where do we go from here?'

I wish I had an answer. If nothing, suddenly it seemed like I had a situation at hand. The rain had disappeared, but the sun wasn't shining either. How could it, when it had set?

⁜

Leap of Faith

NEHA JOSHI

Dear Shiv,

I woke up this morning with a smile on my face. You know how rare that is for me! I thought it would wear off within a few minutes but the infectious little thing was persistent; it stuck on to my face all day. Maybe it was because I saw his face first thing in the morning. He does this weird thing to my insides that force the corners of my lips to curl into a smile. Yes, I know you will say I am lame and cheesy and my life is a sad, sad story. But who else will listen to it but you? I can't believe this is happening to me. I had promised myself the last time that I wouldn't fall into this trap again. Enough is enough. Wasn't the pain Tanay had caused enough to last me a lifetime? But you know my heart and how easily it falls (quite literally). It's been a few weeks but this time, it feels real. Not the together forever types but just, real. I take him for what he is—completely at face value. I don't have any hopes and I have lowered all my expectations, just as you had asked me to. It's strange to think he lives so close by, he has been walking around the corridors of the same college I have for two years but we had to meet only today. Maybe I wouldn't have been ready earlier. Maybe I needed Tanay to hurt me, to show me what pain truly meant in order to appreciate what he has to offer. How else would I have accepted someone who made me pay my share on our first date? All those things that mattered to me earlier—money, status, class—just seem to have vanished. I realize now that what I want is respect and acceptance, things that Tanay could never give me. I'm unsure of this path I'm walking on Shiv. It is cobbled and the stones often hurt my feet. But at the end of the day, he's right there, applying a soothing balm to my wounds and making me feel stronger about my decision, just like you did. He has accepted me, with blisters on my feet and no make-up on my face. And right now, that's all I can ask for, to keep the smile straining my cheek muscles all day. I'm taking this leap of faith, Shiv. Keep your fingers crossed!

Forever yours,
Naina

◆

Dear Shiv,

It's our last night in this world today. No silly, I'm not harbouring suicidal thoughts! I mean this world we have created, our world. We met in this small university town and built our life within it. Our relationship grew here, amidst people and places we now call our own. But today is the last time we will be here; it's the last time we will walk hand in hand outside college; the last time we will share a coffee at the local Café Coffee Day; the last time we will split a 100-rupee parantha and the last time I will sit behind him on his bike, raring through these familiar lanes. Remember how strange it was leaving our home? Silent tears stained our faces as we left behind everything that we had known, those places that had been witness to our bond and us grow stronger by the day. I remember being scared to bits then. Am I scared today? Like hell I am! More than I've ever been. But then I remember something you had told me that evening, as we walked hand in hand through our favourite park in that old neighbourhood. It was a verse by our favourite poet, Robert Frost. *Two roads diverged in a wood and I—I took the one less travelled by, And that has made all the difference.* I'm doing something I haven't ever done before—I'm dreaming a dream we shared, a common dream we had. Yes, you know we've had them before. But we've never lived them. Today, I am. We are moving to a different city, together. We are going to build a life for us, together. I don't know what gave me the strength to make this decision. Maybe I'm just too attached to him; maybe it's the wine I had that night talking. But in spite of these digressions, I've never been surer of doing something in life. Probably that's why I'm so scared! I'm looking at him packing his life into boxes as I write this letter to you. Can you believe he has enough faith in me to put his baggage with mine, and help me open it in a new land? That's probably it. His faith in me, in my abilities and my dreams, that makes me want, to blindly jump on to this moving train of life with him. It's tough leaving this world I know behind. But I can't wait to construct a new one with him, full of hopes and dreams and memories that will forever be ours to cherish. I'm taking this leap of faith, Shiv. Keep your fingers crossed!

Forever yours,
Naina

◆

Dear Shiv,

He just proposed! No, it wasn't at the Eiffel Tower like I wanted it to be. I don't think we have enough money in our bank account to afford a trip to Paris. But it was way more meaningful than I could have ever imagined. Is that what you meant when you said I needed to get real about my fantasies? I guess I have gotten real today. It was a beautiful sight—our apartment was filled with candles and rose petals were strewn across the floor. My favourite music and wine flowed freely as he waltzed me around each room, pointing out things about the space we shared that made it ours. He ended it by saying his life had been intertwined with mine and I was a part of his world, of every inch of his being and of the space around him. The ring was slipped onto my finger and fit perfectly—three diamonds encrusted in a platinum band, just the way I wanted. Of course, he got his friends to light fireworks in the sky the minute I said yes, a spectacle we devoured from our balcony. This gesture scared me a bit. How could he have been so sure of my response to know the exact time the fireworks had to be lit? I'm not denying that I would have said yes any day. But what if I hadn't? I know, I know. I'm overthinking things. I should be basking in the glow this ring brings to my face. It's just hard to accept that somebody knows me well enough to predict my every action.

Nobody else but you has ever been able to do it. But now he can. Are you scared that I'm going to replace you in my life? Hahaha. I can see the smirk on your face. Yes Shiv, you know you were indispensable. Now I have another name to add to that list though. Mom and dad are ecstatic. He has totally charmed them and got them wrapped around his little finger. And you know how tough that is! Mom thinks he'll make the ideal husband because he's so caring and understanding. Dad is just happy he shares his passion for automobiles. They once spent an entire day in the garage modifying the Morris Minor! I never thought seeing mom and dad so happy with my decision would make me so happy. But it does. I guess I had begun to underestimate the power of family after you left. I now need to start drawing out a list of people I do not want to call for my wedding, which is going to be considerably longer than the list of invitees! I'm too excited to be anxious today. But the anxiety will set in, sooner or later. All I know for now is he'll know me well enough to stop me from running away on a horse a la Julia Roberts in *Runaway Bride*. I'm taking this leap of faith, Shiv. Keep your fingers crossed!

Forever yours,
Naina

◆

Dear Shiv,
I told you to keep your fingers crossed! I'm sure you laughed at me and didn't. And see what has happened now? It's all your fault. If you had just listened to me, like I had asked you to last time, things would have been so different. Yes, I know I'm ten years younger than you. I know you always considered me to be an inconsequential meddling kid. But did I really deserve this? Did I deserve to lose the two people who mattered the most to me? He walked out of my life Shiv, just as smoothly as he came in. It took no more than a few seconds. A drunk driver rammed into our car as we were turning at the corner of M.G. Road. The crash was on his side and the impact sent our car swerving across the road, spinning around and straight into a lamp post on the sidewalk. There wasn't too much blood. I just felt his head droop on to my shoulder, the shock I was going through was muffled by my incoherent screams. Life has been a blur since. Everything seemed so familiar; the rush to

the hospital, the sorry faces of the doctors, mom's hysterical sobs, dad's incomprehensible calmness and the flames that turned the last ten years of my life to ashes. I had told him not to take that turn. We weren't headed in that direction. Yet he didn't listen to me and went ahead. Just like you did. If you hadn't gone out that night, when I had begged you to stay home and read Frost to me, all our lives wouldn't be the same today. He was just like you. He probably wanted a new twist to life. And not surprisingly enough, both your actions have landed up twisting my life. I guess that's the price I have to pay for giving you both the right to control my emotions, to navigate my journey; the price I have to pay for loving you both more than I loved myself. I am broken right now Shiv. I have no motivation to get back on my feet and pick up the pieces of my life but for the faith I possess. It's a funny thing, this faith. Once someone instils it in you, it's very hard to let go of. And I had two people believing in me more than I ever did! I wish you had known each other. You were both so similar. But you probably wouldn't have liked him for stealing your baby sister's attention away from you. I don't know what I'm going to do. I can feel the blisters on my feet again. And this time, neither you nor he will be there to soothe my aching sores with balm. But remember how you always told me nothing in life is permanent? Of course you do. But in all my naivety, I somehow forgot. I took you both for granted, never bothering to think how I would cope without you waiting for me with open arms at the end of a tiring day. But now, this journey is mine, and mine alone. I won't ever look back, for this time, I have double the amount of love, hope and belief in me. I will live for the two of you, for the lives you both deserved. For the last time, I'm taking this leap of faith, Shiv. Keep your fingers crossed!

Forever yours,
Naina

Instant Coffee

MONA RAMAVAT

I have sometimes wondered why life can't be like Amma's reliable sambhar recipe.

I don't miss the sambhar, or Amma. We speak twice everyday so it's as good as me being home. But I'm homesick although I'm going home soon. I'm already missing this city which I have made my home in less than a year. And I definitely miss him already. How long ago was it, I ask myself, stirring my cappuccino. Two weeks? That's it?

He'd asked me out two weeks ago.

Have a drink?

I'd looked up from my laptop, hair tousled. He stood at my cubicle, blazer gone finally. Faintly tired eyes taking in my surprise…

I was flattered, mostly because the youngest vice president of the company could awe you, draw you, even flirt once in a while, but he was known to have never asked a colleague out. By Monday morning the buzz on all three floors of the office building was that someone finally had Jatin Srivastava figured.

Amma had just stopped short of having a puja done when I told her I'd turned into a social drinker. What would she say if I told her that I had hung out with Jatin till long after two drinks? It was meant to be simply time away from work after a long day. Relaxed, yet formal. But that one evening had led to another and then another. Four in a row. We actually decided we shouldn't do this for a while. A week later he proposed dinner again.

Can't resist gravity for long...

And what would Kunal say?

Kunal Basu. The nameplate on our neighbour's door was the first thing I saw when we were shifting into our new apartment— Amma and I. After Appa died, I suggested we moved to another place and Amma agreed somewhat reluctantly. We settled down in just a few days and Amma seemed to like our new home except we had a fish-eating, Bengali 'bachelor boy' for a neighbour.

Hi, I'm Kunal.

Hi Kunal. Mitali. Mitali Iyer.

He'd asked us to come over for lunch a few days later.

I'll cook a vegetarian meal, Auntie.

The usual courteous offer to a new neighbour. Amma couldn't stop imagining the supposed veggie lunch cooked in saucepans smelling of fish fry.

Ayyo ayyo Mitali...

I found Amma's attitude towards Kunal amusing initially but then it got increasingly irritating.

Kunal offered to carry my groceries up. I refused. I wasn't sure if he'd washed his hands. Kunal had friends over. They were making such noise! Kunal's phone rings so loud and he doesn't answer for so long. Kunal this, Kunal that! It was getting to me now. So I dropped in at Kunal's one day after work just to see what it was about him that bothered my mother so much.

We chatted for a while trying to be casual on his formal sofa.
Would you like to see my music and book collection?
Sure, why not?

It was a whole fiction library and a thousand CDs not so neatly stacked. He showed me around, sincerely embarrassed about the mess. I borrowed a few and promised to lend him some of mine. Forty-five minutes later we were somewhat more casual.

Amma hadn't been too happy about me 'getting friendly' with Kunal. That's what she'd said. Getting friendly. Going steady. Such terminology was so early last century, I stifled a smile.

By virtue of being neighbours, I couldn't help but see Kunal pretty often. Besides, we both loved music and books. It was also practical to simply ring and ask for a spare screwdriver or last week's newspaper. He helped fix a broken door hinge or deal with electricity bills. Amma suddenly developed chest pains one evening and we drove to the hospital in his car. I had panicked and the only person I could think of at that moment was Kunal.

After the whole hospital episode, Amma had reluctantly warmed up to him but still couldn't get herself to eat at his place. And he wouldn't give up inviting her over, although he knew.

Somewhere in the midst of all the joking and Amma's leg-pulling, those long evening walks or endless games of scrabble, the numerous little things we shared or exchanged on a daily basis, I slipped into a comfortable familiarity with him. And Kunal Basu fell silently in love…

Love. That's a pretty complicated word I decide, dabbing lips with a tissue. Sitting by myself at this practically empty coffee shop in the middle of a weekday when I should be at work is somewhat surprising. Ridiculous too. I sit staring at the hint of lipstick merging with the coffee froth on the slowly unfurling tissue on the table.

If staring could make the minutes tick slower, I could stare on for as long as it took!

The rhythm of Jatin's hands was like a strange spell. He was chopping fruits in his kitchen for our Sunday brunch. His long sun-tanned fingers plus the plain knife slicing through the pineapple looked queerly artsy. The chopping stopped abruptly when he saw me looking. The spell was broken mid-slice. Did I feel stupid? I may as well have picked that knife and chopped myself up if I could! When I finally found it in me to look up again, he was still looking. Rather intensely.

We held hands after long minutes. His, warm and sticky with pineapple juice and mine, slightly clammy. It felt nothing like the countless times we would have formally shook hands in the past. But this was plain erotic. The thought was a bit disturbing. But not very. So that in turn was disturbing.

My otherwise pleasant ringtone cut through the moment. Had to be Amma. It was Kunal.

I wince. The coffee is still pretty hot for a gulp.

After many months of what I could imagine as him preparing for this moment, Kunal confessed. It was a simple *I've fallen in love with you Mitu*. No more jazz than my favourite shade of carnations, on the corridor between his apartment and mine. I had suspected this was coming, but freaked nevertheless. I was not even remotely in love. I was in fact hyperventilating halfway through his revelations.

I was attracted to you even when we first met. I missed you like mad when you were working on weekends. I think I fell in love when I saw you in a sari at the temple with Auntie. Or maybe when-

I shut the door of my home with an angry bang. I switched off from him entirely. This was too weird for comfort. I was guilty too for not reciprocating a love I didn't feel. All in all, it was somewhat suffocating. This whole thing. Even him patiently waiting for me to 'feel comfortable enough'. Amma was most curious about why I seemed so different about Kunal all of a sudden.

Even he kept himself carefully away from me. No more borrowing spare scissors and torch batteries or quick consultations on everything from the most profound to the most mundane. This went on for quite some time, till I ran into him at the supermarket one day. Felt pretty funny about meeting him this way, while he'd always been next door. The awkwardness was so strong that after a while we both cracked up. Soon we were laughing hysterically. Only Kunal could do this. It didn't take long to fall back in the comforting familiarity of his friendship.

We sat by the wayside eatery and I settled for a good talk. It was clearly needed. I made it absolutely clear that I didn't love him. Couldn't imagine myself in a relationship with him. I was also not happy about him ultimately ending up hurt.

That's for me to deal with.

I knew Kunal enough to know that, that was coming too. Had the situation been reversed, I would have flinched. At least.

I was touched with his patience and a love that was turning out to be pretty unconditional...

I look at my reflection on the glass panel lining the wall. A bunch of giggly young girls have walked in. They are now settling at the table next to mine, robbing me of my quiet solitude.

I don't believe I'm rethinking my relationship with Kunal after three years of being in it, counting this one year too when I'm away from home in this other city for work. My relationship with Kunal that I'd spent days convincing Amma about.

Ayyo Mitali! Will it be a Bengali wedding?
It doesn't have to be about marriage Amma!

Then what is it about?

Love? Do I love Kunal?

Two weeks of dating Jatin has made me rethink my relationship with Kunal. Dating? Is that what we've been doing? I don't know, really. Words always taint, don't they? But really, what are we doing? And where is this heading?

Yes, the thought did cross my mind. Many times. But if Jatin was interested only in my body, would he have bothered to open up to me? This much?

It happened two years ago. The legal thing. But it was all over long back. She never was married to me. Her career was her only passion. I loved her... like a madman.

Very few at work knew that Jatin was once married. Nobody knew the details of the divorce. He had the eyes of a man not used to sharing matters this deep. They gave away nothing and simply dug deeper into mine.

I found myself instantly able to share things with him, I couldn't tell anyone else as easily.

How did we cross this bridge? Or did we cross a line?

I've told Jatin countless things about myself in these last two weeks. But I can't get myself to talk about Kunal. Yet.

I can smell freshly ground beans somewhere. My mug is one-thirds full of lukewarm coffee that I don't feel inclined to drink. The chatter and the frequent giggles are drowning out all the silence inside me. Erasing even the faint aroma of the coffee beans, if that's possible.

I pick up a cookie and start munching, for want of doing something.

I had known what the gift was, even before I'd unwrapped it. Chocolate cookies from a bakery on the outskirts. Kunal often brought me these to celebrate a special moment—he tracked anniversaries—to cheer me up sometimes or simply because I loved them. So it was no surprise that I got a ridiculously big box of those to take with me. I was going for a year. Kunal had sort of sulked on and off till days after I told him I had to relocate for a new job. Amma was as apprehensive about staying alone, as she was worried about me going. Didn't seem like such a big deal to me as Amma and Kunal made it out to be. I would after all keep coming over every three or four weekends. Kunal almost made a farewell speech at the airport, chocolate cookie box in hand, and was that a hint of tears in his eyes?

Within six months, my weekend home visits grew less frequent. I had turned busier and also didn't miss home that often I guess.

I'll be going back home in a month. And I don't want to go. Not back to Kunal. Am I getting too deeply involved with Jatin? I don't know. I don't want to.

Three years of Kunal were not as magical as two weeks of Jatin.

The mystical Jatin who could awe and draw anyone but held hands so intimately only with me as though our souls found a way to each other through our enmeshed fingers. He opened up this deeply only with me. Jatin, who I still don't know very much about. Jatin, who was once married and is now divorced.

Two weeks of Jatin have indeed been more magical than three years of Kunal. Predictable Kunal. But dependable Kunal.

I put aside my half-munched cookie. My coffee is a cold, dead pool at the bottom of the mug.

I walk into the sun outside the coffee shop.

And breathe…

ॐ

Collateral Damage

ADITHYA NARAYANAN

'Girl run over by car, dies on the spot, police suspect suicide'

I picked up the morning paper from the dining table with one hand, a steaming hot cup of coffee in the other, and read the headline against the early rays of the sun. It was big and bold, and there was a picture of the accident spot sprawled across the length of the page.

Front-page articles had begun to annoy me of late, I realized. Random, isolated incidents had lately been over-exaggerated and sensationalized in a desperate attempt to catch the reader's attention, and this article was a perfect example of one of them.

A journalism student myself, I had repeatedly been taught in college not to succumb to such editorial pressures and stick to the ideals of journalism. As I stared at the headline, I ran through in my head the faces of my batch mates, wondering if any of them had been responsible for this.

I sighed, put the paper down and switched on the TV. Finding nothing worthwhile to watch either, I quickly finished my coffee and went in for a shower.

Driving to work, I realized, I hadn't thought of my college friends in a long time. After I'd moved into this city, work had kept me busy and I had kept in touch with very few of them. The need to keep in touch with these minimal few also faded away as the months wore on, and it had almost been a year since I had spoken to any of them.

With very little work to do that day, I kept thinking of them all day, and as I drove back home, I decided to make a few calls and play catch up that night.

I sat at the dining table, phone book in hand, and instinctively dialled her number first, only to awkwardly cut the phone even before it began to ring. I stared at the phone and picked it up again, only to decide against it, again.

I was surprised to find out that I was so nervous. The break up hadn't been perfect and I hadn't spoken to her in a long time, but it had been a year now, and I usually handled these things well.

Unable to convince myself to make the call, I gave up and sat back, and let memories of times spent with her flood my mind.

Four years ago, she had been the happiest, most free-spirited girl in college. It had amazed me to see how carefree she was, laughing and giggling with her friends all the time without a care in the world.

Sometime in the second semester, I had asked her out and she had said yes.

Things were good, until her happiness began bothering me.

How could anybody be so blissfully happy, all the time, I began to wonder. Something wasn't right I thought, there had to be something wrong with being happy all the time.

And so, I sat her down one day, and spoke to her about all the things that bothered me. I told her that such happiness was pointless and unproductive and that I wished she did more with her life than giggle and laugh all the time. I began to speak to her about my issues and my problems; about global politics that affected everyone and gave her books to read about them.

It took her time, but soon enough, she began resonating with my thoughts and asked me questions about these things. We'd often have a long discussion, and as time passed, and she began reading a lot, she started finding answers to her own questions.

Her friends began noticing a visible change in her behaviour. She had become very absorbed in her books and she seldom socialized with them.

Her appearance began to slowly change too; she tied her hair in a bun and wore little or no make-up. She began thinking a lot more and started laughing a lot less. She stopped wearing her usual bright colours and wore more of black and white and grey. Her friends drifted away and soon she was left talking only to me.

The fights began a couple of months later. Her new personality had begun to bother me; we began disagreeing on things she never had an opinion on before. As time passed, I realized that she had lost all of her natural charm and colours that had caught my attention during the first few months of college. She even looked unattractive to me, the black, white and grey made her look dull and boring. I began to find reasons to avoid her and we began to drift apart.

I ended it abruptly the next month. The break up took her a little by surprise, she probably thought I'd be willing to work on it, but mature and independent as she had become now, she dealt with it like a lady would and soon we went our separate ways.

I sat up and looked at the phone for a while, and then got up and walked over to the balcony.

Leaning across the railing, I looked across the road, which

I noticed was empty, except for two people who were trying to cross the street.

Their faces looked familiar and so I leaned forward and squinted to see better.

My heart stopped for a second when I saw my own self, standing on the other side of the road. Book in one hand, she was standing next to me and we were holding hands as we began to cross the street. Suddenly, cars appeared out of nowhere and the street became extremely busy. She stepped back, but I seemed determined to take her to the other side and she gave in. We slowly started making our way through the chaos and all seemed well, until midway through I let go of her hand and ran away to the other side.

Stranded in the middle of the road, she looked at me, and then at the other side. The side we had come from had crowded really fast, and she didn't know if she'd fit in there anymore. She couldn't walk over to the other side alone by herself because she didn't know what to do. Completely lost, she dodged a few cars, looked at both the sides and then just stood there looking at me in the distance, before she finally came under a car and blood splashed everywhere.

My shirt soaked with sweat, I woke up with a start and realized that I had fallen asleep on the chair, the phone dangling off the table.

It had been a bad dream.

I looked around the table and found the newspaper lying where I had left it in the morning.

'Girl run over by car, dies on the spot, police suspect suicide', it read.

✎

Pakodas and Chutney

ESHA VAISH

In most Indian households, while Tuesday is the day of rituals, in our house the rituals of Thursday or to be more specific, the all-encompassing singular ritual of Thursday overshadowed all the Tuesday fuss. It began with Ma starting the day furiously chopping, cutting and beating to pulp a number of ingredients in a bid to create a variety of chutneys. The mixer would be whirring furiously, occasionally malfunctioning and spitting up the entire mixture. The twenty-year-old antique was never replaced for doing this; instead Ma would curse under her breath and begin from scratch, employing my extra limbs to help her out. My favourite chore was emptying out the old chutney from the weekly jars. I'd find a rhythm while scrubbing the insides of the glass bottles clean and besides I enjoyed the residual smell of lemon that the dish soap left on my hands.

One would think the persistence with which my mother laboured definitely meant that her mother-in-law was making a trip to inspect her household. However, this was far from the truth. As always, Thursday was 'Neetu Aunty Day'. Neetu Aunty was an arthritis-ridden gossip mongrel, who had lived as our neighbour for fifteen years. Then four years ago, after she almost cracked her arthritis-ridden knees trying to climb to her second floor apartment, her NRI son insisted on her shifting to another building with a lift. He provided the difference between her late husband's pension and the exorbitant price of the luxury of a building fitted with a lift. So, Neetu Aunty wrapped her bulky belongings in tears and drama and moved out of the locality. Owing to her age, she had a huge collection of junk speaking as a timeline for her life and it took the movers several painful trips through Mumbai traffic to deliver her 'precious belongings' to her new doorstep.

Yet, old habits die hard, as did Neetu Aunty's habit of craving for societal gossip. Her sustenance since her husband's demise had been the locality gossip. She'd wrench it out of people's mouth with a tricky concoction of coaxing and demanding. For all purposes she was known as the 'gossip collector of the mohalla' and she did her job with due diligence, displaying none of the lethargy that collectors on the government payroll did.

So to keep herself satiated, Neetu Aunty got a brand new phone installed, the cordless type. Being my mother's good friend, I was relegated the job of travelling to her new house and teaching her how it worked. To say the least, I'd met toddlers who were more receptive. On that trip, Neetu Aunty, to express her gratitude, made gobi parathas and layered them with butter. Amul had sold itself to her it seemed, as by the time she made the walk from the kitchen to the dining table where I was seated, the parathas were floating around on the blubbery yellow remnants of solid butter. However, elderly people are easily offended and the last thing I wanted was a lecture from my mother on manners. So I mustered up my guts and endured the buttery mess.

However, coming back to the brand new telephone, Neetu

Aunty found that it was much easier to pry people's deepest, darkest secret from them over the telephone. The telephone must have given them a false sense of security, or maybe it was rooted in the knowledge that Neetu Aunty no longer stayed in the building, but her closet of gossip grew quickly and swiftly.

She was content with just collecting gossip for a while, but keeping it all to herself gave her stomach aches, the medicine for which she displayed a terrible allergy. So she started making weekly trips to my house to reward my mother, her dearest friend, with her treasured findings. That is how Thursday came to be the day it is.

So every Thursday a cab would be hired and Neetu Aunty would promptly ring our doorbell anytime between 10:30 and 11:00, depending on how she fared with the traffic. Draped in a silk sari, she'd be smiling from ear to ear and thrust a Tupperware dabba of assorted pakodas in my hand. It came to be my untold duty to heat these pakodas and serve them with the awaiting chutneys. During which time, the ladies would make themselves comfortable on our sofa and Neetu Aunty's store of secrets would begin tumbling out. They'd generally begin with the smaller bombs and progressively the exclamations and decibels of responsive emotions would rise. I'd catch snippets of the conversation from my place in the kitchen.

If Neetu Aunty had it her way, I'd be sitting right beside my mother and getting an early training in the art of gossiping, but the first time the suggestion had ventured past Neetu Aunty's lips, my rather docile mother had said a firm and straightforward 'No'. The matter was sealed. Normal conversation had resumed and it was like the matter had never been brought up. Ma was forgiving of Neetu Aunty's unpolished manners and foot-in-the-mouth nature. In fact, she embraced it with the easiness that one would in an elder sister.

Neetu Aunty and Ma had only once had a brief spat when

Neetu Aunty one day had made a snub at Ma, taunting her about Dad leaving us to live with another woman. Dad's extramarital affair was an unspoken matter. It was the toughest struggle of Ma's life and only after many nights of crying herself to sleep had she been able to accept her newfound freedom and the side dose of loneliness. Resetting the alarm clock and throwing out his handkerchiefs was the easy part, the difficult part was eating food with his empty dining chair staring at us, watching as the morning paper lay ignored and other such banal tasks that had marked his constant presence. He'd left to stay in a 'live-in' relationship, saying that she was a much more put-together woman and understood him better.

Ma and Dad's marriage had been an arranged one and the courtship period had been limited to cross-verifying that the two surnames belonged to the same social standing. Within a brief year, Ma had a new address with Dad in a city far from her home. They didn't love each other but they didn't rub each other off the wrong way either. They barely ever fought and I had never imagined my family would suddenly become one person short.

I still remember that day when Dad packed his suitcase, leaving us and his tattered clothes behind, and then there was the day when Neetu Aunty had brought it up. Ma had sliced her mid-sentence and thrown her out with a staunch face. It was only after she slammed the door shut that the hurt surfaced. Neetu Aunty had crossed a line. For many months, I didn't see Neetu Aunty. I ignored her on the stairs and just shook my head and declined her offers to sit in her house when Ma got late from work. I was indignant at the idea of showing any compassion to the beast who had scraped my mother's scabs.

But just like families find it in themselves to forgive one another, mother forgave Neetu Aunty after she shed a bucket of tears and kept bringing guilt-ridden home-made sweets over for a while. Much later in Ma's drawer I found a letter Aunty Neetu had written, apologizing sincerely, a mood that Aunty didn't wear often. That letter choked me up and I realized how much Ma must have come to rely on the support of this lady over the years.

When I asked Ma about the letter, I heard the entire story for the first time. Aunty had helped Ma with the monthly instalments on our flat, even blackmailing her son for the money till he relented. Ma was the reason Aunty had stayed back in the building, fighting arthritis year after year. She would have stayed on forever, but Ma had insisted she find a building with a lift and Aunty had given in. I was touched by Neetu Aunty's devotion to my mother and embarrassed at being brash to her for the past couple of months. However, once the cold war ended, it seemed all was forgotten.

One particular Thursday though, my embarrassment turned into guilt, as I realized that beyond the bullish exterior there was a real lady with real problems. Neetu Aunty arrived as customary at 10:35. But when I opened the door, there weren't any pakodas, just a suitcase. Neetu Aunty's wrinkled face was pale and her eyes were swollen from crying. She sniffed into a handkerchief she clutched in her wrist.

Ma took one look at her and wrapped her arms around Neetu Aunty's large frame. Over a cup of coffee Neetu Aunty narrated the entire story. The time she had lashed out at Ma was to only hide her own insecurity as her son had just informed her that he planned on having a live-in relationship with a girl from his Ph.D. class. She was American. Neetu Aunty wasn't happy but she grudgingly accepted it. Live-in relationships had always made this orthodox lady queasy.

Saving grace, she assumed that her son would marry the girl and the marriage would take part in India. Neetu Aunty was disappointed on both accounts. The son married the girl's previous roommate at Las Vegas. A devastated Neetu Aunty asked for him to arrange a ticket to America so that she could see her new bride. Her son refused, even refusing to continue paying the rent. It seemed Angelica, his new wife, didn't want them to 'squander their money'. Those words were the final insults; Neetu Aunty made the tough decision of disowning her only son. After trying to make ends meet for one month without her son's financial support, the tired lady folded up her dignity and arrived at our house. Ma took her in despite her many protests. Sure, she was an extra mouth to feed, but she was a comfort to Ma and was family. The old lady was grateful and in her I discovered a grandmother who oiled my hair and made me 'all natural' face packs. I loved having her around.

As the years went by, our odd family unit lived in harmony. I graduated with a degree in journalism and fell in love with a young man who frequented the coffee shop near my office. One year into our relationship he asked me to move in with him and I joyously agreed. I wanted to see his face first thing in the morning and I wanted to fold laundry with him. I put my otherwise unblemished happiness aside, as fear crept in of how the two ladies would react. They were all I had and I did not want to distance them from myself.

With trepidation, that day I went home. After dinner I sat them down and poured my soul. All the while, Deepak, the man I intended to move in with, waited under the building in case I needed him around. Both the ladies seemed a little upset and I thought the night would end with much drama. But, once again, they proved to me what family meant. They hugged me and chided me for keeping them in the dark about Deepak. They shared my optimism about the live-in and even invited Deepak upstairs for coffee.

Then the night got stranger as I witnessed that with Deepak, the ladies ended up laughing about their own brushes with live-ins. They seemed to have taken the incidences in their stride and joked about it bravely. I found myself clogged up, unable to cry or smile, just mesmerized by their strength. When Deepak left, I hugged them and cried. I cried in anger towards the cruel men who had hurt these beautiful women. I cried because somewhere I felt I had betrayed them. But Ma hugged me and said, 'Sona, Aunty and I are so proud of you. You weren't tainted by our experiences but accepted them and moved on in your life. Deepak is a lovely boy and you will have a beautiful life with him.' With those words she put my mind at ease forever.

It's been six months since that day and I'm still living with Deepak. Thursdays are still my favourite days. The fresh chutney and pakoda tradition continues. Generally, it is me who visits them in the evening after work with a tiffin full of pakodas. Sometimes Deepak accompanies me. I think Neetu Aunty likes him better than me. For her, I think, he fills the void her son created in her life.

Today, is Thursday and for the first time Ma and Neetu Aunty are coming to my house. It was Deepak's idea to be quite frank. He said that I had put off inviting them home for too long. I was sceptical of what they might think, but I realized he was right. I have prepared all the chutneys just the way Ma used to. As I hear the doorbell ring, I check to taste the last customary chutney, unloading it from the mixer. It's perfect. I can't wait to tell Neetu Aunty and Ma that Deepak and I plan to get married.

༺✿༻

Darling

ARPITA BOHRA

The girl with the lost eyes hasn't smiled today, or yesterday. She's nearly forgotten why she's standing at the edge of the pavement, watching the world rush by. *Stupid me*, she thinks, flagging a cab, remembering.

Today, she has worn her kajal for the first time since *that* day. Now it smudges as she wipes her eyes, waiting for the taxis to slow down, making her wonder why she even bothered when she knew it would come to this.

Minutes away, the man in the yellow shirt is breathlessly pulling his zip up and leafing through his wallet while the wavy-haired woman runs her fingernails lazily down his back. It's a new ritual, and the scrape of her nails through his shirt still sends slight electric shivers through him. 'Not this way!' she singsongs, sulking. 'You know I don't like my darlings throwing money in my face. So many times I've told you. Leave it in the red box on the windowsill like a good customer.'

His phone rings as he slips the last of the thousand-rupee notes into the slit in the red box. He knows it's his wife calling because he'd changed the ringtone to one of her favourites, a song that makes the other woman smirk at him. He doesn't smirk back.

He doesn't pick up, not until he's out—out of the dim heat, the sweatiness, the smoke and smells of lipstick and perfume. Out of her world, and back into his.

In the late summer sunlight, his secrets are bleached invisible. He adjusts his black laptop bag shoulder strap, and presses the phone to his ear. *Such a typical yuppie,* thinks the waiting girl, her gaze resting at the slight protuberance of his paunch. 'Yes darling, I'll be there as soon as I find a taxi. You know how it is in the evenings from this place, taxis don't come by easily.' Something like a smile crosses the girl's face when the stray word sails across the scrubbed steel hum of the hot Bombay traffic to her ears. *Darling,* she thinks. *People still calling each other that. Sweet.*

The taxi driver spits onto the pavement and checks his receding hairline in the cracked mirror and makes a face. He takes out a faded cloth, a green scrap of his wife's petticoat, emerald green the year she wore it at their niece's wedding. He's done wiping when he sees the girl. Dressed in an emerald green salwar kameez, clutching her bag. Waiting. He pulls up, aware of the sudden clatter of footsteps coming from the other side.

'Chembur?' she asks, with self-conscious loudness, as if she is not used to saying the name much. 'Sion.' pants the yellow shirted man. The driver looks at both of them, calculating whether he has time enough before heading back for his daily run to the airport. 'You can sit madam,' he says, gesturing to the girl. She opens the door, gets in, and pauses.

'Does Sion come on the way to Chembur?'

New to the city, he thinks.

'It does.'

The girl glances at the other man stepping back, squinting into the distance. She thinks about the person he just called darling, and how it used to feel when someone spoke that way to her. And unexpected words fall out of her mouth before she can keep them inside.

'If you wish, you can sit in the front with him, and we can split the amount till Sion.'

For a moment, he says nothing. And then smooth, crisp, words glide out of his mouth in self-assured English.

Are you sure? Yes? Thank you. That would be good. Thank you.

The taxi driver adjusts his mirror so he can see her, slightly. She's not from Mumbai, yet. He can tell. It takes time for the nervousness to mellow into nonchalance.

She slumps back against the seat, and closes her eyes. She hopes the man in the front seat doesn't think she wants to make conversation, or swap numbers. She avoids people who want to get to know her better because she knows how difficult knowing her has become since he left. The last of the hazy sun is setting and she only wants to be able tell the man who loved her about how the peach light is falling like silk over the bruised grey walls, making the world feel like a painting, for a perfect moment. But he's not here anymore. He turned into air and smoke and earth and water and the ash in the locket around her neck, while she was waiting for him to come back.

'Haan, darling. Guess what? I just found a cab. I'll see you in less than an hour. Sure. Love you.' The girl lets out a long sigh, and fumbles in her bag for her sunglasses, feeling the same treacherous feelings again. Weddings do this to her. People holding hands do this to her. Even overheard, everyday flickers of affection do this to her. She wishes she can go back to a time where she enjoyed these things. Such unexpected bitterness, she can feel herself rusting from it, no matter how hard she tries not to. From his rear view mirror, the driver wonders at the sunglasses while the man turns around to face her.

'Thanks for sharing the cab. As it is, they are really difficult to find on that stretch of road. I appreciate it.' She smiles a small, non-committal smile at him, and nods, grateful for the sunglasses. Wanting to say simple, everyday things like 'you're welcome'. But they're out of reach today.

She watches him fill up the silence with a voice supple with happiness, curving around the city and politics, as he chats to the driver. Looking at the aged, bitter face of the driver, she wonders if the old man has ever felt that kind of softness in his own voice. If he has ever called anyone's name with the kind of emotion the other man says 'darling' with. If he has known tenderness, known love, known what it feels like to be stretched to breaking with loose, sunny joy because of someone else. And before she knows it, she's sailed back into a memory. How it was raining the last time she was here, here with him. Outside the blue blur of the taxi windows, the world stood still while the rain fell, quiet, impassioned. How gently he held her hand, in that familiar way of his. Every single time she looks at her hands now, all she can remember is how he held them.

Sometimes, on the harder days, she wishes she could forget and un-remember all the memories she is made of, because keeping them inside makes it so hard to move. But only for a moment.

'Hey uncle, I'm just returning her the favour. Here's Rs 200 from my side. Don't charge her more than Rs 100 now! I know the rates to Chembur very well!'

'Haan-bhai, haan,' the driver says, gentle and vexed at once. 'Don't worry about it bhai. I'm not going to cheat anyone here.'

He grins contritely at the driver, and clambers out of the car, pressing his phone to his ear. He mouths 'Thank you' to the nodding girl, who wants to say the same to him, for paying more than her share. But strangely, her gratitude sticks in her throat again. As the car moves ahead, she watches his lone figure shrink from the side mirror, envying the person waiting for him, so sure of his return. Then her eyes fall on the hands, gnarled and knobby, clutching the steering wheel. Faded scarlet rakhi threads are wrapped like straggled promises on his wrist. On the other wrist, there is a yolk yellow LIVESTRONG band. She wonders who bought it. And she remembers more than she'd like to. Before the world blurs with memory, she decides to try and make a run for it. Across the tightrope which holds both questions and answers together. Simple, predictable ones, the kinds we all have answers to.

Where. When. Who. What.

Not *why*.

Never, ever , why.

Banaras.

Twenty-five years ago.

I have a wife and two daughters, Rashi and Seema.

'Who gave you that yellow wristband, uncle?'

Meena, he says. But not out loud. He adjusts the mirror, thinking and sure that little sunglasses, for all her sweetness, would never understand such love.

'Oh this wristband, my daughter Rashi gave it to me—a Neil Armstrong band, she told me. You can do anything, anything, if you can be strong. She's wise, that girl of mine.'

The girl notices how his smile slinks into his voice as it talks about the yellow band and its giver. *Love* she thinks, *proud love*. His daughter is lucky her father has eyes for specialness. But *a Neil Armstrong band*?

'So how much do you earn?'

'Twenty, twenty-five thousand a month. So much goes for the education, tuitions for the girls. You can get cheap classes, but I want them to have the best. And my wife does not work outside.'

Like a lover, he wants to tell her about how hard his Meena works, at the airport, cleaning the bathrooms. How her tired face always lights up when she sees him come to pick her up. How much he wants her to rest since her last viral attack, and how she always shuts him up and cooks him dinner, every day, though he knows the fevers left her finger joints sore and swollen. How badly he yearns to take her out for a meal, but never seems to have enough money to spare without some kind of guilt.

How one can only eat so much vadapav.

How Ms Sunglasses, with her smooth English voice and her bag full of books will always be able to enter worlds which his own daughters might never be allowed to walk through.

He thinks about the jobs Meena gets refused because she doesn't have any papers. *So smart and so wasted. How she cleans up after the hard-eyed ladies in high heels and lipstick. 'It's the way they look right through me,' she'd told him once. 'Like I'm a part of the bathroom, like the sink or the shit-pot. Not like I'm one of them. That's what makes me mad. You better make sure Rashi and Seema never have to live this way.'*

He shakes his head and declares loudly, 'Education is the only way to get yourself out of the muck of the world's dirty jobs. Without English and education, we're trapped—working only where no one else wants to. You people can work in neat and clean offices with ACs and keep your hands clean while others get them dirty.'

The girl, whose mind is always unravelling the ways of the world and trying to knit them back in softer ways, wants to tell him how no clean white office can take away the pain of losing someone. How it hurts so deep and hard that nothing else seems worthwhile. How sometimes she feels that being loveless is more frightening than being poor. But she keeps quiet. Sometimes she's sure that the truth is never the same for anyone.

'You educated lot, you can afford simple things that are big for us. You can go to a restaurant without thinking too much about money. We can't.'

'You're right,' she says, sighing.

The clean, spicy scents of the small vegetarian dining hall Meena always gazes at when they cross it, come back to him. Rs 200 for a thali. She has wanted to go there forever, but she's never let him take her. Rs 200 is half a month's subject tuition for Rashi, she says in her simple way. And he finds it hard to disagree, simply because it's true. But it's also true that she cares for his daughters more than their mother does, more than they know. Sometimes, he's surprised at her goodness. He tells her he doesn't believe in God, as much as he believes in her.

The taxi finally reaches Chembur. The meter reads Rs 300. The girl gets out, and gives him Rs 500. He sees the money and takes out Rs 200, checking to see if there are any people on the usually deserted side road, and decides quickly. *It won't hurt her.*

'What's this?' she asks when he gives her Rs 200 back. The quaver in her voice makes him more confident. 'Madam, you had to pay me Rs 300.'

'No I didn't,' she answers. 'You've been paid Rs 200 of that amount already. Give me my money back.'

'That's not the point.' He makes his voice louder, because it's easier to feel righteous when he shouts. 'You came by meter, went by meter. It says Rs 300. You let the man share the taxi, which was kind of you. But you still owe me Rs 300 for the drive. You've paid and I've given you your change back.'

The girl's shoulders slump. *Thank God*, he thinks. *If she was the kind to fight I'd have been in a tight spot.* 'Uncle, you know what you're doing isn't fair. You've taken Rs 200 more than you should. Give my money back.'

'Listen, that passenger paid for his trip, and you pay for yours. The truth is that I dropped two people off, not one. It's my taxi, and I can decide who pays me what. And you can argue till tomorrow if you want to, but I'm not giving you any money. You've paid for your trip, he paid for his. End of story.'

She begins to repeat what she was saying but he looks away, at the road, ignoring her, shaking his head and beginning to shout 'I don't have time to argue, madam. As far as I know, I dropped two people, and I collected two fares. Bas'

The girl is pleading, not outrageous. Kind of like his Meena is. She doesn't know how to fight, either. 'This is not fair uncle and you know it.' She whines, over and over again. He thinks she might even cry, and he decides to leave without saying much.

'Listen I'm tired of all this, madam. This is Mumbai, and I don't have time to sit and argue pointlessly. I'd have earned a hundred by now. So I'm telling you now, you go your way, and I'll go mine. Bas.'

The girl takes off her sunglasses and he sees her eyes flash with anger and sudden tears. 'Fine!' she shouts.

'You know what you did, and you'll know too when it comes back to you. Your Sai Baba won't be able to protect you then. You'll understand how little it was worth fighting for.'

And then she turns her back to him and walks away.

For a few silent moments, the taxi driver feels stung. *She's right,* he thinks, wilting. He watches her retreating figure vanish faster and faster and is gripped by the sudden urge to run back and return her the money. But then he remembers Meena. He sighs and looks into Sai Baba's brown eyes, perpetually glistening with compassion. 'I'm sorry about this. But you understand me, and you understand why I did this Baba.' He looks at the face earnestly; long enough until he is sure Babaji is convinced.

Driving along the highway, he grins broadly to himself as he presses his grubby phone to one ear, waiting and willing her to pick up at the other end.

'Darling,' he drawls, 'Be ready. I'm coming to pick you up. And today, I'm taking you out to dinner.'

Slut

HINA SIDDIQUI

She was walking down the street, her satchel of books slung across her shoulder, the strap pressing against her thin t-shirt, her skirt swishing unceasingly between her uncaring feet, and her eyes flitting mischievously from one site to the other of the world she could conquer.

She was a girl, and though her bra strap showed through and her skirt threatened to Marilyn Monroe with the next gust of wind and though more catcalls and leering glances came her way than the girl wearing a hijab who was walking with her head duly to the ground just across the road, she was a girl, just like every other girl. She could argue about Ibsen with just as much gusto as about an episode of *F.R.I.E.N.D.S*; she could nod her head to *Guns 'N' Roses* and shake her hip to item numbers and perhaps make the best coffee this side of Thiruvananthapuram. She had grown up in a place where her parents didn't just speak of equality, but offered a fair taste of it, where the decisions she made mattered and if a man thought he could get away with things just because he was, well, a man, he was politely asked to sit in a corner and rethink his strategy, because egotistic belligerence, though very 'manly', was going to get him nothing.

She walked in to a run-down chai shop, where once upon a time, she had failed to notice in her modest absent-mindedness, that every heterosexual male within range treated his eyeballs to her figure. In that oblivion she had continued to visit this place, which was cheap and comfortable and allowed possessions of seats for much longer than they were strictly needed.

And thus, the men became used to her presence, though they did try to get a good look into her shirt every now and then, they had been largely desensitized to her presence. Even so, she was asked to readjust the way she sat once in week or so. She walked to the table in her favourite corner, smiled at the boy who was sitting in her favourite place, then shrugged and made do with the vacant seat closest to the spot she loved. She pulled out a book but found her mind dissipating off the page like the smoke from the cigarettes around her. It was a day of distractions and the air smelled sweet.

Chai shops, especially ones that have been around for generations without having changed the price of their cutting, have this uncanny ability to inspire reminiscence and thus, when memories gathered at the door, she sedately bid them welcome. She remembered the first time she had met him, she still hesitated to call him a boyfriend or anything as impersonal as that. Just this morning someone had brought it up in college...

She wanted to scream. Not just scream but tear the entire library down. Rip the useless books to shreds, putting an end, once and for all, to the outdated theories they propounded, punch the nose of the lascivious librarian all the way into his retarded brain for wanting more to get a better look at her chest than help her find the reference material she needed and finally, blow the entire bunch of morons who had set this assignment on her in the first place to little smithereens which she could then watch floating away with the breeze while enjoying an apple popsicle on this summer's day straight out of hell. However, knowing full well that she had pretty much condemned herself to typing out pointless pieces of information every now and then simply by joining an expensive college for a fancy degree, she kept the angst to simmer, kicked her flip-flops off and marched to the nearest dust-mote infested corner of the library to make peace with the futility of education. And it was then that she stumbled over, quite literally and not to mention painfully, on what could very well be the man of her dreams. Not that she wasted time dreaming of men, those blissful mirages were occupied very much with images of travel and career, but had she been thus inclined, he very well could have been part of that fantasy world.

He sat there, his curls hanging over his forehead, biting his lips, his eyes still pouring over the lines of a battered copy of Dante's Inferno, oblivious to the fact that he had just been the cause of the latest in a series of mishaps in a particular girl's day, while the girl herself lay spread-eagled at his feet knowing not whether his curls deserved more attention or the guitar leaning by the bookshelf on his side. The crash was followed by silence, till he said, 'You really should watch where you are going,' and that too, without even bothering to look up.

'You really have cute hair,' came her reply.

He didn't offer to help her, merely got his feet out of the way. He didn't take her for coffee or even intend to. She didn't ask him for his number or even bother to give him hers. But they sat there, by the dusty shelves in the fading summer sun, talking about literature and science and music and history and all the things that mattered to them, for well over four hours. And by the time the library shut, their conversation had just begun.

It was good that she was young. Any older and that memory might have faded. They had lasted all the way through the first year and well into the second and were still going strong, still talking for hours on end, still getting to know each other and it was still fun. A man walked in, not one of the regulars, and as such made a point of staring at her very intently. He chose to sit right across from her and she chose to ignore the obvious implications of his leering. Something similar had happened not too many nights ago. They were at a friend's birthday brouhaha at a popular drinking hole, where people that young weren't really allowed but got in anyway, and everyone she knew was somewhere or the other on the scale of tipsy to so-sloshed-I-need-assistance-to-go-to-the-bathroom-to-throw-up.

She had worn something strappy and short, for that was the theme, heels, because they went with the outfit and red lipstick for the first time in her life. Frankly, it wasn't the kind of thing she'd invest in most of the time, but this time it was different. There was a thrill in being looked at and admired, even envied and maybe, just maybe, she'd get a high on that today instead of just booze. She took in the compliments, saw, from the corner of her eye, people she had never noticed before— boys smiling a little too broadly, licking their lips, girls making faces, sniggering, then lowering their guiltless eyes, watched as boys fell over themselves to get her drinks and smiled when her boy asked politely for them to get him one too. And she enjoyed it all.

Till the man walked in. He sat at the bar, ordered a stiff, then another, ate fistfuls of peanuts and all the time, he stared at her— watched her dance, watched her laugh, watched her drink—adjusting his trousers way too many times to be considered decent. And when she needed to take nature's call, he followed her.

There was no reason why a bathroom at a bar needed to be so far away and secluded. Perhaps the proprietors thought that people needed utmost seclusion after drinking away their pay cheques or in this case, pocket money. But the walk was unnecessarily long and poorly lit. And it didn't help when Creepy Letch came along and tried to strike up a conversation.

'So you hang out here often?' he opened.

'Yes.'

'I haven't seen you around much...'

No reply, not that he got the hint.

'I like your dress, it's sexy.'

A weird look, not that it made a difference.

'You look very good, you know. I can see you are a bold girl.'

Now these would just be cheesy openers, but the man's slur, his lowered eyes pinching her, and the fact that he was now close enough for her to see the smoke stains on his teeth made for a very uncomfortable situation. She tried to back away, but he blocked her. Without thinking she pushed him and just as instinctively he grabbed her, around the waist. She tried to knee him, but she was too close to aim. She struggled, but he pinned her against the bathroom wall. So this was what it felt to be an animal in one of those squeeze cages. He pressed his mouth against hers...

And she bit him. Very like the animal in that cage. And ran.

A funny thing happened that day. A random stranger assaulted her, could have done worse if circumstances had not prevailed, and the next time she walked into college, she realized just how much people who weren't there seemed to know what exactly had gone down since they had been texting, Facebooking and meeting ever since. The worried eyes, the angry frowns, the sympathetic arms, the concern, the cajoling, it was stunning to find out that unbeknownst to her that so many people cared so much about her. They had even come up with a special name for her.

'Slut'...they called her. And synonyms and metaphors and colloquialisms in between.

Boy, her boy, had heard the rumours and when he met her that day, he looked at her for a second, held her hand and asked,

'Do you need to go to the doctor?'

'No,' Slut—well, since they had christened her, so why not—
replied.

'Do you want to talk about it?'

'No.'

And even when she felt safe enough to return to the scene of
the crime and relive in third person what almost too many girls
have to go through in this world and what most of them earn a
label for, she knew that she didn't have to explain a thing to him.

The man kept staring at her. Only this time she stared back.
She dared him to try something.

He didn't.

And that brought her to this morning, the memory of which
had churned this whole day into being.

She had walked into college, fake friends had said, 'Hi!' and
hugged her tight, shoving their bosoms into her face for the want
of a better way to rival her.

Poseurs had asked, 'So, what's the score for this week, huh?'
giving her a wink like it was all in their stride.

'Zodiac: 37, SFPD: 0,'... she had replied, tapping her nose when
confusion—the only genuine emotion ever played out on their
faces—shone through yet again.

And then someone came running, the same someone who
incidentally, everyone believed her to be cheating on her boyfriend
with, and issued a summons to the principal's office.

*Principals, no matter what veneer of open-mindedness and
progressive thinking they throw on to suit the institution that currently
employs them, are basically the same under the graduate robe and
obscure degrees. They are manipulators of a system, nothing more or
nothing less, and though their intentions may be good, what else is
the path to Hell paved out of? Slut had realized this when she was in
school, but since voicing such opinions didn't change a thing, it was*

her own private joke. And thus, she was smiling when she entered the venerated man's office and even the scowl on his moustached lips didn't ruin her humour.

'Why?' he asked coldly, looking straight at her.

'Because sometimes you have to,' she replied, with a calmness that would annoy lesser mortals.

'I didn't ask for rhetoric, I want an explanation.'

'People are welcome to judge me—call me a poseur, a rebel, a delinquent—in their heads. They pass their opinions about me within hearing, I'm going to have my say.'

'So you thought the best way of having your say was to slap a fellow student in class?'

'No, I said what I had to, during the open forum in class, till the teacher asked me to shut up and took his side, you know because— why not?—and then dismissed my theories based on nothing, again, because... why not? I said I had the facts to prove it, she interrupted me, told me to sit down and get my facts straight.'

'And what did you do?' he asked, dripping sarcasm, but having no effect whatsoever.

'I sat down.'

'And then?'

'She asked me if I had understood. I said "yes". She asked me again. I said "yes". And that's when he laughed and turned to his friend, who was cozying up next to him, and said something that I overheard. So I turned around and... I guess you know what happened then.'

'What did he say to his friend?'

'He didn't tell you?'

'No.'

'Then why should I?'

The principal had considered her for a moment and let her go. Slut walked out of his room and out of the college, out to celebrate; she had called him to meet her on the way out. And as the events unfolded in her mind, he sat there, beside her, on her favourite chair in her favourite corner of her favourite chai shop.

And he smiled.

'Slut'...they called her. And synonyms and metaphors and colloquialisms in between.

And as she sat there, with a fresh cup of tea, holding hands with someone who she didn't need to explain things to, Slut realized, she finally didn't care.

hardly stepped out, instead eating lunch and dinner with whatever was available and sleeping through the mornings. He had liked the way in which the last two days had passed.

But now he had to rummage and finding nothing readily edible, he stepped out, maybe thinking of going to a restaurant. Indeed he'd had his lunch in a restaurant, but he wanted to take something back so that he wouldn't have to trot out for dinner as well. Thus he went to the grocery at the corner of his street.

The busy grocer was shouting out for his assistant to go buy something when he went there. The poor fellow almost tripped as he rushed out.

Saleem tried to smile at the grocer. He knew him.

The grocer eyed him suspiciously, but then recognizing him, hailed him and started chit-chatting as grocers usually do. It was a hot afternoon and it made one talk dreamily of nothing in particular, just to ward off the drowsiness.

'You never come here anymore! You buy from the supermarket isn't it?' he complained, whether for fun, Saleem couldn't gauge.

'No, bhaiya!' he protested, 'I don't live here anymore, no. I live in the hostel. Summer vacations only now.'

And suddenly the grocer took his eyes off him, steering them to a genial alertness on a point just behind him.

'Bhaiya, one kilo onions, please, fast,' said a voice rapidly from behind Saleem.

He turned back trying to place the accent.

When he looked at her face, he stopped thinking. It was Shabnam.

After all these years.

His heart skipped up, hurting him a little. He let out a low whisper of joy. But her face registered no recognition. Maybe she didn't recognize him. It hurt him to think so.

But it seemed like she hadn't seen him properly, for when she did, her face assumed a wondering expression as if trying to place him. His heart skipped up again. He decided to go for it.

'Remember me? Saleem!' he exclaimed pointing to the scar on his wrist.

'Saleem!' she cried, recognizing him, 'It's been such a long time! You've grown so tall, I promise!'

She held his hand, looked at the scar and smiled sheepishly.

'I caused that, didn't I?'

'Forgiven!'

He smiled at the ease with which he could talk to her. Now that he had seen her, he remembered the longing he had often felt for her back when they were in school.

'What are you doing now?' she asked.

'Engineering. Vacations now, two months. Where do you stay?'

She told him the place.

It was quite near his house. He suddenly grew excited. No one was home. She was not the orthodox kind of girl, he knew. Maybe he could invite her over. They could discuss the long years they had not seen each other. She had grown so beautiful. Maybe she felt for him the way he used to for her. Or rather, like he was feeling now.

'My home is quite nearby,' he started. He didn't want to sound wrong.

'Here are the onions, anything else, madam?' cut in the grocer, smiling.

He wanted to kill the grocer then.

'No, thank you and my husband will pay as usual,' she said, turning towards the grocer, smiling.

'Okay. Hey what did you want?' added the grocer to Saleem.

'Nothing,' he said blankly. Everything came crashing around his ears. She was married. That's why she's here, he thought. She'd moved to her husband's place.

'What were you saying?' she asked Saleem.

'Nothing,' he said blankly.

'You must come see me some time, I'll tell Farooq what good friends we were. Farooq'll like you.'

'Yeah.'

'Nothing?' the grocer was bemused.

He had not gone to her house. He knew Farooq slightly.

Saleem saw her. She was there. Why now? Why was she in the supermarket?

She was not the supermarket type, he knew. Warmth and care she would want, not the automaton she'd meet at the counter. She needed a grocer to talk to. To tell him that her husband would pay, as usual. She needed his smile. He instinctively knew it was so. Though he hardly knew her, he knew her well enough to know it was so.

Then he saw him, her husband. Saleem started getting away. He would eat at the restaurant. The faceless waiters would have to do.

As he was walking away, she spotted him. He hurried off faster, acting as though he'd forgotten something outside. She couldn't shout of course, but she tried waving at him. But he slipped away as if he had not noticed.

She stopped waving and he could see her talking to a puzzled Farooq. He was out at last. He didn't want to be introduced.

He thanked the supermarket and the corporate retail invasion. What he wanted most had been given him—cold, commercial space which lent him the distance to lose himself from others.

৩৩৩

Noxious Emancipation

KIREN JOGI

Hop skip jump, hop skip jump. Now I'm running. I stop. I refresh myself with an ice cold bottle of water. It burns its way down. Hop skip jump, hop skip jump. The sweat is dripping. Run... faster... run. It's not sweat. My eyes are moist.

She has these weird notions. Therapy is what she calls it. I call it punishment. Each time there was heartbreak she followed a vigorous routine of torture. 'It's a process of reaching enlightenment,' she'd tell me. I'd be confused but pretend to understand. It was easier that way.

In the two years that I've known her she has inflicted this craziness upon her at least five times, if I'm not mistaken, and that too for the same fucking guy!

It started off with this guy called Rahul. Apparently, she wasn't good enough for his parents. He ended up getting hitched to his boss's daughter, whose toilet paper factory he worked in. I wish I had been there for her then. I know it sounds corny but I would have been the one wiping her tears.

And then the dancer boy, what was his name... Vicky. If it

wasn't for him I guess we wouldn't have ever met. I liked him. This wizard turned her world upside down. Literally! She ended up trading a career in the police force for the so-called world of 'glitz and glamour'. I mean, come on, any bastard who can hypnotize you into leaving a secure career of chasing criminals in exchange for a life of chasing casting directors sure has to have some magical powers. Think about it, what would you choose? Knocking from door to door with a loaded gun in your pocket and being offered tea and biscuits or knocking from door to door being welcomed by some casting couch sleaze wanting to get into your pants? Hmm.

Oh hang on. She's just woken up. She looks weak and pale. She's trying to smile at me through all those pipes attached to her. Oh fuck! I hate this. Not having control. I want to take her away from here. To a park. We can hold hands and walk on the morning dew. The first time I met her was on the grass. She was lying there in a white night dress that was rolled up to her thighs. An angel fallen from the sky, that's what I had thought. Yeah I know! Totally corny or a cliché, whatever you want to call it! There was a springy ringlet of hair across her face that waved in the breeze. I'm smiling to myself. Then she rolls over on the grass. Now she's a mud monster. I think that's what I love about her. She's so unpredictable.

There's a strand of hair across her face right now, I'm smiling again! *You can light a whole cricket stadium with that huge smile of yours, kid! A whole stadium!* She always tells me that. I end up blushing like a chick and then she comes over and drops a peck on my cheek. I try and control myself but it usually makes me hard! I hate that. Not having control!

She's sleeping again. 'There is something about the smell of hospitals that slides you straight into depression,' she'd tell me. Hospitals being one of her most-visited hotspots. I can definitely vouch for that right now. Don't think I've felt this depressed since my assassination on the school bus. You see I'd been attracted to this girl whom I'd pretty much stalked all year round, and in my defence you should also know that she was aware of my prowling and encouraged it to a certain degree, so before the summer vacations I plucked up the courage to sit next to her on the school bus. We sat nervously glancing over towards one another. In all that anxiousness I sneezed en route her face, knocking her out for a six. Slightly deluded by the happenings, she stood up in shock only to realize I had sat on her skirt and there she stood in her floral panties. That tight slap she sent my way only added to the roasting my face was undergoing in all this embarrassment. That mortification on the bus only led to sheer depression, which then led to a summer phase where I hid from my friends and stayed locked indoors.

This depression is different. I guess it's matured. School bus, school crush, hospital, love? The hospital is where she met her next love. This guy was perfect for her. Gulp. I am the perfect one for her. Dr Manu was what she called him. He was her therapist, who she went to after she tried slitting her wrists when the wizard, Vicky, decided to perform a vanishing act on her. Dr Manu was the type of guy that cooked lobster on Valentine's Day served with champagne, whisked you away on exotic holidays and took you for a horse-carriage ride along the riverside, and all that jazz. And then she fell out of love with him because he was too perfect. I guess she wanted someone who'd push her around, give her a few bruises. You see in life you always want what you don't have, but what you have today is part of yesterday's desires. The human mind is a greedy predator. Never satisfied, I tell you. That's probably why women like bastards; they're always making them crave for more.

She's been my prey from the first day I met her. She has this command over everyone she meets. Her aura entices you instantly.

At least that's what happened to me. Shot me straight in the heart. Yeah, I'm wounded.

After that morning, when I saw her passed out on the lawn in the compound of the building we stay in, I helped her in her half-drunken state to her flat. That afternoon I stood there by the window just watching her, she was like an empty canvas. I wanted to paint this picture so desperately. And in that desperation I stood there trembling as she walked towards me. I froze. I'm telling myself to move, to say something that will save me from this goddamn embarrassment and of course my school uniform not helping me out in any way. I'm too young to control these sexual desires you see. But she caught me in the act. Yes, one hand on my penis and the other wiping away the sweat that was erupting from my face. She came over and bluntly stared at me. The silence was deafening. I swear I felt a whole lifetime fly by—that was the level of intensity. And then all of a sudden she burst out into a fit of laughter. I must have turned bright red. I could feel the heat slapping my face. And then she said, 'Thank you for bringing me home.' Aah! It all sounded fuzzy and I bet she could see the stars that were dancing around my head, like they have in cartoons. I'm watching her right now as she sleeps. If I ever saw the men that did this to her I would kill them—with the support of some kind of weapon of course. She always tells me my scrawny body can't even tackle a fly. She's the best thing in my life right now. And it fucking hurts to know it's not gonna last. She's slipping away and there's nothing I can do about it.

If I became prime minister, I would blow up all the alcohol factories in the world. Maybe I should join al-Qaeda or some kind of terrorist group to do that. Truth is I'm not blessed with an IQ level to rule the country.

Since we moved in next door I've watched her pour poison

down her throat each day. Don't get me wrong, I did try God knows how many times to make her stop, but it was always too late. See, the last relationship crushed her world completely. To be frank I would feel the same... I think. She left a home, a family, a great career and moved from Shillong to Mumbai, only to learn that the person all these sacrifices were made for, decided to walk out on her after six bloody years! Is this what one calls karma? She did leave the perfect guy for this piece of trash called Shiv, who turned out to be gay! Yep, this is the guy she would repeatedly torture herself for, with her so called 'therapy' routine. I really feel for her.

You're probably wondering how I know all of this, right? See, I have been her confidante since we shifted to Mumbai with my huge family from Bangalore. The family never really noticed I was missing, even though the nine of us including my grandparents and brother, two sisters, chacha and mom and dad shared an eight hundred square feet dingy flat. I mean, come on! Lord, have mercy! How do you expect me to focus on my studies while my grandparents are snoring away in the hall, my younger brother is trying on my mom's saris (I'm sure he is gay) in the shared bedroom, my chacha is surfing the net for porn instead of jobs and my two sisters are copying dance moves from a dance reality show on TV. Oh and I forgot, my mother is fighting with my maid over why she comes to work for five days and takes two days off every other week. Hold on, isn't that the case for everyone in Mumbai? I guess that makes us ten in totality then.

Math is my weakest subject. She would tuition me every alternate day. Sometimes I could smell the alcohol from her breath when she'd lean over my shoulder to check my calculations. I would make mistakes on purpose so she'd stay there a little longer, trying to figure out where I went wrong. I tripped on her fragrance, in addition to the strands of her hair that fell on my face, minus the

Supermarket

T. NANDAGOPAL

Saleem was back home for the winter. He was now in a supermarket calculating what he could take back to eat.

The cold, detached shopping appealed to him now. He could get away from anyone he knew. And with a little effort he could even go through the entire exercise without talking.

The aisles seemed familiar enough though he had never been here before. The detachment of the shopping experience held him in thrall. The noise, the people without faces, the lips behind the counter which wished him a nice day though they couldn't care less, the whole supermarket in fact, prefigured in his imagination as the loss of his own expectations. It had all become a part of the drearily moving machinations of his life.

He remembered with fair distinction the last time he had been to a normal grocery store. He couldn't forget it actually, though he'd been trying to.

Six months ago, to the date, he had been hunting all over the kitchen for something to eat. The usual stock of eatables had been diminishing mainly because his parents were not home. He had alcohol breath of course and plus the sweet fragrance of her hair, she always had my undivided attention. We'd have breaks in between. This was her time, I would listen to her as she would pour her heart out. Sometimes she'd make me a mango milkshake or open a packet of cookies. On milkshake days when she'd turn on the noisy blender, I would shout out, 'I love you!' from the hall, she'd pop her head out from the kitchen oblivious to what I'd said and wait for me to repeat. 'Nothing,' I would reply. She would put on her confused face and continue to whisk my favourite beverage. I loved these games. Oh God! The machine is beeping! 'nurse... nurse!' I'm shouting at the top of my lungs! Where the hell is everyone? Don't panic, don't panic, it's all gonna be okay... 'Nurse! Doctor! Anyone! Help!' I'm sweating holding her hand. I don't want to cry. Not right now.

A doctor bursts through the door. I can't stop the tears. I'm standing speechless, just pointing towards her and the beeping machine. I think there is someone escorting me out of the room. My legs feel like jelly. I can't hear the beeping anymore. 'She's stable,' the doctor's telling me moments later as he walks towards me in the corridor. I'm relieved. He's advised me to call her family. I'm scared. I walk back into the room. I've got goose bumps and I'm sweating. My body is playing games with me. To be more precise, God is playing games with me. Surely he is. Okay, let's analyse this situation. A sixteen-year-old boy falls in love with the girl next door, a girl who has fallen in love one too many times, and as a result has fallen into the trap of drowning her sorrows in alcohol. The boy picks her up from her fallen state on the lawn of his compound, only to learn that this fallen flower cannot be revived in any way because she's slowly but surely falling into the arms of death. Get real people, God is playing a game with me.

The past twenty-four hours have been a roller coaster ride. I can remember brief snapshots. Painfully. We skipped tuition yesterday; she seemed quite rough and had already consumed half a bottle of vodka. She was in a nostalgic mood. She just wouldn't stop talking about that jerk, Shiv. I sat there trying to figure out whether she could see the jealousy that was raging inside of me. Obviously not I concluded. The alcohol was too potent. She would spend time writing when she wasn't under the influence of heavy drugs or alcohol. That was a form of release for her. That's what she was doing yesterday when I entered her flat. She was slouched against the divan on the floor, occupied in her thoughts, writing. There was sandalwood incense that was burning and the long curtains were battling against the wind. It was like a scene from a tragic movie. I wanted to hold her so badly. Damn. Let her crumble in my arms and allow her to remould herself in any way that pleased her. She looked at me helplessly beckoning me to come to her and heal the pain. I walked towards her and picked up the bottle of vodka from her side. She tugged onto my hand and pulled me towards her. I was nervous, but did as she instructed. As I sat down beside her, she opened her notebook and began to read.

Abducted...

You held me hostage in your alluring world, infusing your
trace through every nerve,
Slowly but surely invading me whole, you raped my
innocence, you smudged my soul.
Yesterday's fragrance I failed to find... YOU, you have
programmed, inside my mind,
What was I, who was me, you erased my past so
ingeniously.
Obliviously I surrendered my all, you dictated yes, you
pledged control,

Blindly I agreed, saw eye to eye, my mistake, so here I cry...
Trapped and naked I lay down in your arms, why did you
deceive me? Why did I believe thee?
You burnt the warmth, it's cold and bleak. The smoke, the ashes,
I'm smouldered and weak.
A poignant aftermath, I celebrate my liar... question... how could
my love so simply ceasefire?
Our remains I hoard, like a desperate being, these images
I keep tragically seeing,
Haunted by his charming blast, the scars, the wounds, the heart
smashed,
Courageously I struggle to emerge, to leave him, to return
to me, so I myself submerge.
Oh seductive slayer, hither I prayer,
Permit me to perform this toxic release, the ache the niggling,
it has to cease,
Though the heart forbids me to make escape, the mind rejects
this emotional rape,
So here I declare this gratification, goodbye my love, accept
my noxious emancipation.

She cried. And wept and cried some more. Never in my eighteen
years have I ever felt so helpless. Immobilised, I sat watching my love
disintegrate bit by bit. STOP! STOP! STOP! My heart screamed.
Not being able to watch this sight, I walked out the door.

What if? What if I stayed back a little longer yesterday? Maybe
she wouldn't be attached to all the tubes right now. Maybe I will
never know. I'm so fucking angry with me right now. Wait... what's
that noise? It's beeping again. She's opened her eyes. Oh my God!
She's looking at me, the way she did yesterday, she's calling me.
She's smiling. I'm smiling too. I rush over to her and hold her hand.

She's trying to say something, her eyes are weeping. 'No! Please don't say anything!' I'm telling her as my heart pounds a million beats a second. 'I'm begging you please don't say anything just rest, please.' She smiles and closes her eyes. Beeeeeeeeeeeeeeeeeeeeeep.

'Doctor! Nurse! Someone, please help me!' I'm yelling. There's an army of white coats that charge into the room. I don't want to let go of her hand, she's still holding me. I can hear voices but nothing makes any sense. It's all a blur, I can only hear the tears that are streaming rapidly down my face. My hand is pulled away from hers. The people in the white coats stop. No one is doing anything. 'Help her! Help Her!' I'm shouting. ' 'PLEASE HELP HER!' I'm pleading. They all leave, all but one who walks towards me. 'No! No! No!' I scream and run out the door.

Hop skip jump, hop skip jump. Now I'm running. I stop. I refresh myself with an ice-cold bottle of water. It burns its way down. Hop skip jump, hop skip jump. The sweat is dripping. Run... faster... run. It's not sweat. My eyes are moist.

It is therapy.

༄❀༄

If Only

SRINIDHI RAGHAVAN

A car ignored the red traffic light and sped across the junction near the Thirumalai local railway station. A man in his late twenties reacted a second too late and got hit while attempting to cross the road. The red hatchback stopped for a few seconds longer but then vanished into the quiet evening. The man with help from a stranger managed to make it safely to the footpath. After catching his breath, Aarumugham dragged what was sure to be a broken leg a kilometre away to his home. His wife rushed to the door to see the blood-stained lungi. She called for an auto and took him to the hospital. The doctor expressed the need for a surgery to insert a metal rod to fix the broken leg. Aarumugham and his wife, who had two children under the age of ten to bring up, couldn't bear such an expense. He only drove a rickshaw for money and she was after all, a domestic help. Their combined salaries only just managed to meet the basic amenities of the family of four. They couldn't afford an operation which would easily be a few thousands. They stared at each other for several uncomfortable moments before politely refusing. 'Vera ennapannamudiyum?' asked Arasi. The doctor, understanding their situation, bandaged his leg and told him to not put pressure on it for a while. He solemnly explained that the cast will be permanent and that Aarumugham will not be able to drive a rickshaw again. Two weeks passed by, Aarumugham couldn't move at all and was compelled to watch as his wife cleaned up after him in addition to her already heavy workload. Torn by guilt at his helpless state and the futility of the situation, he approached his wife and sorrowfully said that it would be best if he left home and went away instead of being an added burden to her. Her face dropped but she didn't correct him or attempt to hold him back. Tears rolled down her flushed cheeks. She was at a loss for words but knew his mind couldn't be changed.

If only.

In another part of the city, at another time...

The local trains in Chennai were an excellent way to get around as well as get to know the city intimately. For a non-resident with little ability to bargain, it was also an economical mode of transport as the auto fares tended to be atrocious. In hope of a relaxing day spent wandering and getting lost, I left my tiny apartment to catch the 10.40 a.m. local from Velachery, heading towards the beach. Chennai as a city was always somewhat of a mystery to me. While growing up, I used to come here to visit my grandparents during my summer holidays. But back then I never really cared to explore the city. Moving back many years later to work as a veterinarian at Blue Cross gave me the opportunity to get better acquainted with it.

I hummed a tune as I bought a return ticket to Mylapore. I took a seat in the nearly empty ladies' compartment. I stared at the peanut shells on the floor as I waited for the train to be on its way. For a Saturday morning, the train was not unnaturally empty. I pulled out my copy of *The Old Man and the Sea* and settled into the wooden seat by the window. The city was perpetually hot and in the monsoons it was usually humid. But as the train began to move, the breeze cooled me down. Hemingway's words enveloped me as the train chugged along. Soon the need to stand by the door and watch the city go by overwhelmed me. I dropped my book into my handbag and stood by the door. The trains didn't move very slowly but slow enough to capture a gist of the city. I allowed myself to take in as much as possible. The trees, the thatched huts near the stations, the piles of garbage on the roads and in empty plots, the sights of cars that looked miniature from the high train tracks—all painted a picture not too different from every other urban city. Despite the similarities, Chennai's air felt different to me. Perhaps my experience of the city will always be influenced by its relation to my first attempt at being independent.

As we stopped at Kasturbai Nagar, a soft beautiful tune being played on a flute drifted to my ears. I turned around to see a young boy between the age of ten and twelve in the compartment. He was dressed in a pair of torn shorts and was shirtless. He looked at me after much hesitation and asked, 'Song play?' I nodded in approval. Despite knowing the local language Tamil, I was still hesitant to converse in it. He went on to play a beautiful tune that I couldn't quite place but it sounded innately familiar. His eyes shone with hope as he played the tune that evidently came naturally to him. After rehearsing the lines in my head, I asked, 'Un peruyenna?' He was taken by surprise and didn't hide his emotions at all. He smiled as he said, 'Ramesh, akka. Neengo?' 'Swathi!' I said, excited to have struck a conversation with him. Assuming the conversation had ended, he sat by the door and continued to play his flute. I sat opposite him and allowed myself to get lost somewhere between the notes. After a precious few minutes I questioned, 'Engai kathinday?' 'Naane vaasichipathein' he replied, explaining that his mother also plays. 'Romba nannairikku', I managed. Just then, I noticed that the train was pulling into the station where I had to get down. I smiled and waved at him as the train sped away; he reciprocated with a lot more warmth than I expected.

As I headed towards the much-talked about book store on the streets of Mylapore located right under the skies, my thoughts revolved around the soulful tunes of the flute. I was delighted to bear witness to the oldest librarian who shamelessly nudged me towards the back of his collection where the classics were stored. The piles of old beautiful-smelling books were enticing and soon I was oblivious to the world around. I snooped around for a while, thrilled about building a collection for my home which has been inhabited by me without any books for a good six months now. It was an unbearable delay on my end or as my mother calls it 'just plain procrastination' to get out and shop for the treasures. The sight of books with price tags of Rs 25, Rs 60 sent me soaring. I bundled up books worth over Rs 300 and bounced out of the shop. I decided that since it was only a little past 12.30 p.m., I could wander around a little before I ate some lunch. The very thought of getting lost in a city that I didn't know too well got me excited. I have always felt that one can learn most about oneself in times of absolute helplessness. In that moment, I remembered the tunes played by Ramesh. They had a sad yet hopeful feel to them. I felt ashamed at how often I was ungrateful for the privileges I indulged in. I wondered where Ramesh lived and how small or big his family was.

As I meandered meaninglessly lost in my thoughts, I almost tripped on a man lying on the footpath. He began to apologize profusely in Tamil as he struggled to sit up. He was dressed in a white sleeveless t-shirt and a lungi with a checkered pattern. 'Illa. Illa. Naanpaakalai,' I said quickly. My eyes fell on his broken leg which was in a white cast. Embarrassed, he turned his face away and waited for me to leave. Something about him made me want to talk to him. 'Yennaaachu?' I asked, pointing to his leg. 'Accident', he replied. I asked him where his house is and he responded that since the accident he couldn't even go to the bathroom and had left his home behind.

I asked hesitantly, 'Pasikarda?' He nodded his head. I walked away and found a bakery nearby. I bought five vegetable puffs for both of us to eat and sat down next to him and handed him three puffs. Calmly, I pulled out mine and began to munch. He took the hint and followed suit. We ate in silence for nearly ten minutes, following which we sat in silence for another few minutes. Finally he said, 'Yen peru Aarumugham. Ongaperuyenna?' 'Swathi,' I replied. The silence crept back and we didn't even look at each other anymore.

I glanced at my watch without being too obvious and noticed it was 1.45 p.m. It was surely time to be on my way. But I didn't want to leave abruptly. He was quick to sense the unease and said, 'Ningo poganum . Yenakku teriyum.' I held out my hand for a handshake but he didn't oblige. As I walked away he called out, 'Akka, neego ennikana inda side wandenglana, wanduparungo.' It was my turn to nod, albeit sheepishly. I walked away slowly and conscious of holding his attention till I turned the corner.

As I waited at the train station, I couldn't get my mind off the two strangers I had interacted with in the same day. I imagined myself in either of their positions and wondered if I could still manage to be hopeful. Would situations of extreme desperation not turn me bitter? After all, Ramesh was still a child and definitely not the only one of his kind. The sound of the tunes he played, haunted me all the way home. I wrapped myself in my dupatta in hope to generate some warmth. But instead, the world around me—the sounds and sights evaporated as I drowned in the power of the humbling day I had, with the music of the flute in the background. Aarumugham must miss his family painfully, I thought. Much like I miss mine right now. But at least in my case, there is the hope of visiting and reuniting. Did he harbour similar hopes or had he surrendered to his fate? If he had, was that really such a bad thing?

The day replayed itself in loop in my mind; it was a random day that made little sense as it left me confused. If only I could help either of them.

As darkness fell and the hard work for the day ended in a corner of the city...

Ramesh ran into his thatched home with his flute under his arm screaming, 'Amma! Paru naan evalo konduvanduirukkin!' His mother hugged him and put food on a plate for him to eat. She stashed the money away under the earthen pot in hope that someday he wouldn't have to play the flute for money. She ruffled his unkempt hair and kissed his forehead. After his modest meal, Ramesh sat outside their one-room house, under the starry sky, and played the flute. His mother fell asleep with the tune soothing her.

ॐ

Breaking of Innocence

TEJAL JOHRI

I was only eleven when Amaya married a tall, long-haired man with an amicable smile and the gentlest of eyes. He gave me an affectionate pat on the head, and gently brushed his lips with my crimson cheeks before he left with my sister.

He must not have known it, but he was the first man to kiss me. My father was a good man, but he paid more attention to the fish he caught than to me. He said I was a nuisance. I knew better. It wasn't hard to put two and two together to see that my black eyes, my straight black hair, the tiny dimple on my right cheek and my skin the color of snow reminded him of mother. She died in childbirth. I do not remember how she looked but everyone in this village thought I was much like her, if not a shade lovelier.

I grew up crying on the shoulders of my sister who used to spend sleepless nights holding me in her arms, gently rocking me while she sang to the night birds and the wind. The moon must have been mesmerized by her voice, for it was never curtained by clouds when she walked back and forth in the verandah. She taught me what rain was and why it came late. When the sand castle that I had built after hours of tedious work was washed away by the waves of the ocean, she spoke at length about the erratic mood of water. She taught me how to braid my hair, how to catch and cook fish, and how to read. My father was of the opinion that I would learn more at home than at school. Amaya thought otherwise, but took it upon herself to be my teacher.

When she left, I sensed such a morbid emptiness in my heart that I would spend days sitting on the rocks at the beach with my legs in the water. I let the wind play with my hair while I cried my eyes out and my feet got numb in the icy water. I felt lost, helpless and without a friend. I missed Amaya and prayed for her to come back but I knew it would not be so. She had a new life with the gentle-eyed man, while I was stuck grieving over fond memories of the past.

Late one evening when the orange sun seemed to have given up on me and was retiring into the heart of the ocean, my eyes fell on an absolutely ordinary sight—a boy helping his father with the day's stock of fish. Tall and lanky, he must have been fifteen. As he heaved crate after crate from the boat onto the wagon, I sat admiring the leanness of his muscles and the tautness of his skin that was darkened by hours of tiring work at the sea.

I was captivated by his broad shoulders and the sweat that trickled down the sides of his forehead as he drew the boat out of the sea. I was tempted to dive into the depths of the chocolate pool that his eyes were.

His eyes were on me. I had been staring.

Embarrassed, I looked down and began fumbling with the ends of my blue skirt while they worked. I allowed myself a tiny peek at him and found his eyes studying me. Scared, I ran back to the confines of my four-walled hut. I wanted to talk to Amaya.

I was so intrigued by him that I stopped feeling miserable about being lonesome. I thought of my sister's husband and of his gentle eyes. Then I thought of the boy at the sea with the chocolate brown eyes, and I felt a warm, fuzzy feeling gushing inside, that sent a blush across my face.

I asked my father if I could catch fish with him. People in the village who saw us walking together to the beach must have thought I was a very nice daughter to be helping my old father, but I had my reasons for wanting to be on the beach. I was disappointed for I did not see him that day, or the next. On the third day, he was there just like I had seen him before, heaving crates with his father. My heart skipped a beat. We worked for two dreary hours in the sweltering heat. I stole glances at him while he was working, all the time dreading the thought that he too could sense them.

Two days later when my father left me alone at the beach, I struggled to pull the boat out the sea. One edge seemed to be stuck in the mud. I was losing hope when all at once two masculine hands grabbed my hands from behind and tightened my grip on the rope. The mud gave way and the boat lifted itself up onto the sand. I was silently overjoyed for I knew it was him who had helped me. I turned and gave him a smile of gratitude. He inched closer and his fingers grazed my thighs. Then he left. I stood standing for the next ten minutes on the beach, trying to understand what he did and why. I felt a tad embarrassed but I could not understand why.

Amaya would have warned me of what was going to happen, but then if she were there, it wouldn't have happened in the first place.

I had begun liking my work at sea. It was strenuous but it gave me an odd sense of satisfaction, as if there was a reason to haul myself from the bed at dawn. I felt alive and relished the small fish I had for dinner. After that strange encounter, I was unsure of how to approach him, though I was certain that nothing wrong had happened.

Once it started raining heavily. I saw the grey clouds darken the sky as they cast a shadow on the churning sea. A storm was approaching, and soon the waves would take us all inside if we stayed there. I looked for my father but he must have left. Scared, I looked around in desperation and found myself being dragged away from the water forcefully. It was him, my chocolate brown-eyed boy. Relieved, I let him take me up on a small alcove formed by black rocks on the edge of a cliff where we would be safe from the waves. It seemed big enough for ten people.

I was completely drenched and shivering from the cold.

'Thank you.' These were my first words to him.

I saw him studying me again, and suddenly the alcove was too warm. He came and bent over, and started putting my hair away from my face, behind my ears. He hadn't said a word to me till now and somehow it seemed that he wouldn't. I wanted to tell him so many things, but he seemed more interested in making me dry. He wiped the water from my neck and off my blouse. I did not understand why he was so concerned with me being wet, and then he tried opening my blouse. Feeling awkward, I resisted but he forced it open and moved his fingers over my chest. I was too young to know what he was doing, but I knew that he was hurting me. I saw the look on his face and it scared me so much that I started crying. Then the look was gone, and he saw me with those chocolate eyes again that seemed frightened and confused. They were asking for forgiveness, begging me to understand that it wasn't his intention to inflict any pain or resentment on me. But then he got up and vanished, I don't know where. I curled myself into a little bundle and cried. I thought I had found a friend. Who was this monster? My innocence was broken, and no one could help. Not even Amaya.

Palace Dweller

SNEH THAKUR

The view from the highest floor of the palace opened out to a city enveloped in an orange dusk. Birds created patterns in the sky as they flew back to their resting places. Dim yellow lights appeared like dotted stars in the city below as people readied for the night ahead. It was the kind of view that only princes and royalty were blessed with. But in an abandoned fort the only person who laid eyes on such beauty was the fort's watchman, Ghanshyam Singh.

Ghanshyam walked along the dusty corridors making the last checks of the night. His strong, wrinkled hands nudged the rusty locks on the doors to confirm they were locked.

A flock of pigeons cooed and fluttered their wings, nestling into the high, arched windows.

'Arre, chup!' he scolded the birds and as though they understood, they quietened down. A sad smile crossed his face as he ran his fingers along the wall's blue, stained tiles. Moisture formed in his cloudy blue eyes. The recent news had unsettled him.

Deshpande, the new security manager had called him to the lawns to break the news.

The site was to be renovated into a hotel. New, spiffy teams of butlers, security guards and customer service personnel would be brought in to provide a 'royal' experience to the guests.

'Ghanshyamji, the government is very thankful for all your years of service,' he said as he handed Ghanshyam an envelope.

Ghanshyam's chest swelled with pride, 'There is no need for this, saab. It's my duty.'

'Yes it certainly was. But you see, the government has awarded the security of this mahal to my agency,' he said, rolling a coin over his fingers.

Ghanshyam smiled, mesmerized with the little coin trick, 'Oh that's great news saab. Come let me show you the main storage. You know, in the rains...'

'There will be no need for that Ghanshyam,' Deshpande said, kick-starting his sparkly red bike. 'You have until the end of the month. The envelope has enough for your way back home.'

And with that he revved the bike and sped away, the thud of the bike matching the frantic beating within Ghanshyam's chest.

◆

What Ghanshyam called home was a small, functional room in the backyard of the fort. A yellow bulb dangled precariously from the ceiling on a thin wire. Against the south wall was a wrought iron bed which he folded up during the day. A steel trunk with 'Ghanshyam Das Kumar Singh' written in blue lay on the floor. The trunk was like a versatile actor in a play, sometimes doubling up for a table where Ghanshyam would place his chipped cup of tea. And sometimes making a handy albeit uncomfortable seat on which he could sit to slip on his sandals. While Ghanshyam found this way of life perfect for his humble needs, his younger brother Yuvi would often complain.

'Bhai, in the daytime the light is too harsh and at night we can barely see under this bulb. The guards in that City Hotel have cable TV and fans and here we are bitten by mosquitoes each night. We should go back to our village, to our land. That's where we belong.'

'And what about living in a palace Yuvi?' Ghanshyam would remark. 'Look, look outside,' he would say nostalgically, sighing at the sweeping views of the palace grounds.

'Remember, we came here all those years back. Just you, me and this palace. Even the school on the right came after us.'

'But Bhai,' Yuvi would complain, 'why do you want to work in this abandoned fort? Ramji said the land prices have sky rocketed back home. We can sell a little and set up a shop. Bhai, we can even buy a new Yamaha bike and show that Bhushan Singh that we are not poor but richer than him!'

Ghanshyam would smile fondly and shake his head, 'Silly boy. Don't you understand? We don't need all that,' he would say.

'We live in a palace. We are like princes.'

◆

In recent years, the government had commissioned a school near the palace. Every morning like clockwork, hordes of children would gather at the grounds for assembly. They would read out the news and school events for the day. This, Ghanshyam would hear with great interest. In the age of TVs, which he could neither afford nor watch due to his cataract, it was the children next door who introduced him to the world. As they wrapped up assembly with the national anthem, Ghanshyam would join them in the singing, his booming voice suddenly melodious and proud.

There were some mischief-makers of course. Young boys who would wander into the grounds with their girlfriends, trying to steal a kiss or two. And the cricket enthusiasts whose shots would end up dotting the palace with several tennis balls. They all knew Ghanshyam and relied on his good humour to not complain to their principal. In return, they would indulge in his stories about the history of the palace—of a time gone by, when the corridors were vibrant with festivities and colour.

But what was to become of him now? He was just an old man with a lathi. Vijay, across the street who was in the same line of work as himself, had learned how to drive. But the expenses on the cataract surgery had rendered this option useless. After years of working in menial jobs, carrying sacks for the Seth and sweeping roads, he had found something that he could take pride in. This was all he knew. This was home.

♦

The palace grounds wore a desolate look. A dried leaf rustled, breaking the silence. The early morning prayer had just begun at the school assembly. Ghanshyam pedalled slowly towards the main halls where he was to meet one his successors.

'Dada! Here!' a voice yelled out to him. 'You seemed lost there. I don't blame you. Look at this place!'

Ghanshyam walked up looking diffident. The boy in front of him was young. He had a carefree way about him in the way he stood, hands dug deep into his pockets.

'My name is Vivek,' the boy said, finally pulling out his hands from his pocket and stretching them out for a handshake, 'But my friends call me Rocky.'

Ghanshyam took the boy's hand hesitantly. He was surprised by the firm handshake. Vivek sat down at the low steps of a main hall, reaching for a loose cigarette from his pocket. He looked so at home that Ghanshyam felt like their roles had been reversed—he, the new uncertain recruit and Vivek, the more experienced guard.

'So Dada, how long have you worked in this,' he said waving his hands at the expanse, 'place?'

'About thirty years...' Ghanshyam said, absent-mindedly counting on his fingers.

'Ho, ho ho... thirty years! In this banjar?' Vivek flicked the ashen flakes to the side of the steps.

Ghanshyam's mind went to the slowly receding cigarette. 'I was twenty-four when I got this job.'

'Dada, it's your time to rest now. Why bother with this lonely fort? Go home and let your children take care of you, correct?' Vivek stood up dusting the back of his jeans.

'Deshpande sir wants me to start on the 5th. You will move out by that time I'm sure. I will bring my bags on the 4th. Now Dada, take me on the grand tour.'

Ghanshyam nodded his head slowly and gestured for Vivek to begin walking. His gaze was transfixed at the fading remains of the cigarette butt now littering the ground. Instinctively, he bent down to pick it up and slipped it into his pocket making a mental note to throw it into the dustbin later.

◆

Ghanshyam broke the news to Yuvi and told him about the new guards. To Ghanshyam, these men seemed soulless. Always dressed in black, like death itself. Dark glasses never letting anyone see the eyes behind them. Their voices robotic over the handsets they spoke in to.

The 'top security agency' had taken no time in combing the fort and assigning their men. It amused Ghanshyam to think that a fortnight ago, it was only he who guarded the palace.

'Wah Bhai, your one job is now replaced by ten new guards. Is this how they repay you?' Yuvi said bitterly. 'They have the money to bring ten more, so why can't they keep you? After all these years…'

Tears welled up in Ghanshyam's eyes. Did they really have no room for a man who had spent his life within these walls? Maybe if he stayed a while, they could see that he could do the job?

He decided to not lose hope, 'Don't worry Yuvi. I will talk to them tomorrow to let me keep my job. We gave our life to this palace. It will protect us.'

◆

On the morning of the 5th Ghanshyam wore the lone black kurta he owned. This, he reserved for special occasions. He didn't own black pants or a black shirt, the dress code of the younger guards, so this would have to do.

He cycled to the main grounds. The halls had begun to show some early signs of restoration work. He smiled involuntarily. Oh to see the fort restored to its original glory!

Vivek saw Ghanshyam pedalling towards him from a distance. He felt somewhat embarrassed, not knowing what to say to him.

'Dada! How nice of you to come and say goodbye,' he said without much formality.

'I am not going,' Ghanshyam answered.

'Not going?' Vivek laughed. 'And where do you intend to stay, Dada? As you can see, there is a new team now.'

'They can keep me. I know the fort. I can help.'

'Dada, you are old. This is not a suitable job for you. Go home. Go rest,' Vivek remarked.

Ghanshyam flinched. He stared into Vivek's sunglasses catching a dark reflection of himself, angry and old. No, this could not be. This would not be. He would not let the palace go.

Then in a voice which wasn't really his, he snarled, 'My name is Ghanshyam Das Kumar Singh. Not Dada. I have guarded this fort for thirty years, much before you saw the face of the earth. For thirty years I cared for this fort. Look at the walls, look,' he said pointing a shaky finger, 'not a scribble, not a single scribble.'

Ghanshyam moved towards Vivek, 'You young guns think that I am old? I am useless? Tell me to go home? This is my home!'

Vivek was stunned by the sudden change in Ghanshyam. The man that stood in front of him was no more the kind-eyed palace guard. In his place now stood a man trembling in anger, blue eyes ablaze with a manic look.

He tried to put some authority into his voice, 'Look, Da... Ghanshyam, it seems to me that you are getting angry for no reason. This is not my fault.'

Ghanshyam mimicked him, 'Not your fault? You didn't so much as speak to me properly. Flicking around your cigarette like this is a dustbin! Calling this a banjar?!'

His loud voice had attracted the attention of the other guards nearby.

Ghanshyam was not finished with him yet. 'Your Deshpande thinks he can hand me an envelope and that's it? Thirty years within a small pocket of paper! Here, I don't want your dirty money,' he said forcefully, handing Vivek the envelope.

And then suddenly as though all the anger he had spilt had depleted him, he hung his head—resigning to his certain fate. He picked up his bicycle and walked slowly towards the main gates to leave.

Tears rolled down his face as he muttered quietly to himself, 'This is my home... my home.'

◆

No one could recognize the fort a year later, that shocking was the change. Graceful fountains had sprung up in the alleys. A new coat of paint cloaked the walls. The sounds of restless birds were replaced by the quiet calm of hotel music.

The neighbouring school had been instructed to stop the morning assemblies to avoid any inconvenience caused to the hotel's elite guests. On many a winter evening, the fort would be lit up in much grandeur for a high-profile wedding.

The only aspect of this manufactured beauty that was not in symphony with the rest, was the regular sighting of an old man strolling outside the palace gates, talking to himself. If you asked the palace guards about the old man, they would tell you about his once glorious past. Of how he had come to work in the palace after having lost his only younger brother in the riots in his hometown. Of how he had guarded the fort for thirty years before he was asked to leave. And of how his broken heart had never healed.

You would see Ghanshyam drag his old, tired body across the road to gaze at the hotel.

And if you heard closely you would hear him say to himself, 'Look Yuvi, at our palace. Didn't I tell you—we are like princes.'

From Mother to Son

ANANT TRIPATHI

My son, how lonely I have been.

You never knew me or I, you. They say a mother always knows her child, for she grows him as a part of herself. You were born from my body, but I cannot claim to know you. In my mind you are like me. I do not will it, but the image of you always seems to have my small nose and the slant of my eyes. I have no way of knowing if my mind's eye sees true but I believe it does not matter. It gives me something to grasp however, a mould to hold my son in my heart.

Even now, I imagine you as a dark-haired boy, with a quick-growing body, and your father's hands. His hands were ever so strong. I recall how I remained so fascinated by his fingers. Long and veined, they were always cold on the tips. You must be growing a beard, like him. How I loathed its coarseness, but he would never shave it, only trim it something fancy. A beard will suit you I think, just like it did, him…

I cannot focus these days, not for long. I am weary of writing, my son. I wish I could see you and say to you all that I need to.

But I forsook that luxury years ago, in another time, and I cannot simply wish it back. So I must write, but pardon a dying woman if her words jumble and lead her astray... I am writing in snatches, between food and sleep. There are times when pain seizes me and I cannot hold a pen. But I dare not go back on my words, or erase a letter, for I fear the next moment. I fear I may be lost and...

I am better now, and my mind feels steady. A letter may only communicate one way, and I have little time to waste over my old-woman's rambling, and so I think I will put my will to sketching myself to you. I will tell you all about myself. I will give you everything, to possess as a memory or a portrait to judge me by. You are my son, and this is the one gift I could ever give you, so the decision of how you'd keep it is yours to make.

I was born in the summer of 1961 in New Delhi. My parents were Nitin and Stuti Khanna and my father lovingly named me Ishani after his grandmother. We were the most modern Punjabi family of those days. My childhood was spent simply though, imbibing idealism and discipline from my father and finding joy and love for life in my mother. I find that much of what they taught me then has shaped my adult personality, even though my choices were always mine to make. I had a very normal and wonderful childhood and it remains to be the most innocent, most beloved of my memories.

When I was fourteen, I went to Doon to study. My father had been promoted to general manager and his posting was in the hills. I was excited and left my childhood home without a tear. Only now do I find it strange that I never felt a pang of loss, but only excitement and thrill. I have always welcomed change, always been fixated by newer things to explore and adore. I think it has ever been both my gift and curse.

So I was in Doon for the rest of my schooling. Today I believe those years shaped me into who I am. I was a good student. I aced all my subjects in my first exam making both boys and girls at my school jealous and wary of me. But I had always been good at making friends with strangers, and soon I settled down. I also played tennis. My father had abandoned his love for cricket in pursuit of education during his teenage years and I think he never forgave himself, the curbing of that passion. But he made sure to let me find my sport, and I found both intrigue and pleasure in tennis. During my Doon days, I spent hours in the court every week, exhausting myself to dreamless sleep on some nights and wearing my skirt a length shorter than normal when the boys came to watch. I played seven state-level tournaments and won two titles during that time. I recall how proud it made my father and how happy he was.

In my third year there, I also let a boy from my tennis batch flirt with me and even held hands with him. I cannot recall his name, perhaps it was Kush or Ketan, but he was a nice boy, fair and curly of hair, and all the girls liked him. On our first real date, he tried to kiss me, but I did not let him and fled. I recall thinking about my foolishness the entire night and cursing his awkwardness all the while. The next day, when I went to him with only the need of getting kissed again, he was shy and distant, like a stranger.

I think now that I had hurt him, and his distant way angered me as only girls are angered. It was a bitter parting.

In my last year at school, I had a whirlwind romance. I received a letter one morning. It was kept under my desk, and I only found it later in the day during the lunch hour when I went for my bag under my desk, thinking of food, and something fell out of the compartment. I would have dismissed it as another of my wayward notes if not for the colour of the paper. It was pink, perhaps meant to catch my attention or because Ritesh liked it. I never asked him.

But it was the first letter he wrote to me, the first in a series of extensive treatises on my dazzling charisma and my endless charm. He was a new boy, from my junior batch, and I only discovered him one day when he came to collect a letter from me. We had been sharing letters for a month and in my last letter, I had told him I would come with my reply at the usual spot and not leave it for him but sit myself beside it, if he so chose to come to me. I waited for an hour, but he did not show up. He did come, however, and only when he was sure I was gone. But I hid behind a wall and saw him pick my letter and read it several times while standing in one spot. I had known. I had seen the boy looking at me in school several times, and even taken note of his high cheeks, sharp nose and wide shoulders more than once. Suddenly his gawking was alright, even flirtatious.

I recall his stupid grin as he read it, so like my own when I received notes from him. Once or twice, he almost danced or laughed in joy. I cannot say exactly what it is about written communication that thrums the heartstrings between lovers. I think it is the effort one takes to shape the thoughts of love into inked words.

I did not reveal myself to him that day, but only a few restless days later, when I finally mustered the courage. I strode up to his classroom in the middle of lunch, having been unable to eat mine because of the butterflies in my stomach, and shouldered my way through the throng of his friends and stood before him. Once I was there, I suddenly did not know what to do. 'Hi,' I said, stupidly. He looked at me and suddenly his face lit up. He stood awkwardly and said, 'Hi.' To this day, it is the strangest and the most cherished memory of him I have. He was so adorable, so human and so unsure of himself. That tongue-tied reply from him eased the tension and before I knew it, I was laughing. He stared for a moment, clearly embarrassed, but started grinning as my amusement continued. We skipped school after that and had the evening entirely to ourselves. I sat with him under a great tree on a hill near my school and we shared time and affection and laughter and slow knowledge of each other. At some point, he kissed me that evening, but I cannot clearly recall when.

From there on, the days flew and so many beautiful memories were made that I now wish we had had more time to make them. We would skip school and spend the day walking, talking and discovering each other. I was shy but he would always find ways to steal kisses from me. Soon I started dreaming of making love to him, having his children. It was not long before he started talking about those things. Perhaps that should have been my sign. Love too strong needs determination to uphold. But we were young, and youth is for mistakes.

We quarrelled once, and then again, and there came a time when it was all we did. There was only so much space our egos were going to yield and none of us could bear such frivolity from the other. During one of our nightly conversations, in exasperation I suggested we each take a breather from the relationship. Not touch each other, not speak to each other, and not meet for a while. His ego did not let him refuse. We did not talk for a day and it made me lovesick, as I am sure it did him. I almost rang his phone but did not. The next morning, my head was full of anger and I did not call him out of spite. He must have thought the same things of me, I think. We kept our promise that week, and continued it. After a month, I had resolved to push him out of my mind. In two, it felt like I had.

Love is easy to lose. Its memory does not die of course, but wanes. Promises do not become false, but fail to retain relevance. So it was with mine. In retrospect, I could say we were foolish, that we were kids; that I regret the decisions we made. In fact though, I do not. Those decisions have made me.

It is funny how life goes in circles many times before it finally comes around. We changed cities again. I came back to Delhi to attend college. Life did not mend immediately, but it persevered and set itself aright. I had found a new place again, even if it were the city of my childhood. I made friends. Friends became circles and I became the centre of these circles. I studied philosophy and compiled a thesis on rhetoric in political discourse which I am still proud of. I travelled all over north India and found a hobby in Kathak. There were a couple of casual flings too, but it was not the stuff of legends. I graduated, completed my Masters and my Ph.D. Before I knew it, change set in again, and as always, I welcomed it.

It was at my first job that I met the man I would later wed. I got a job at the university, starting as the philosophy replacement. Amrit was the sociology replacement. Even though I kept hearing about the passionate new sociology professor from my colleagues and students, we never crossed paths until a month later.

I had been a little late for lunch, and arrived in the faculty mess to find my spot already taken. I was too tired to wait and not in the best of spirits. So I carried my plate to the students' mess, looking for a secluded spot. Instead, my girls caught sight of me and I was dragged to a heavily crowded table. That was the first time I met him. Not really 'met' him, since we were not introduced and we did not talk. But as he sat in the middle of a throng of ladies and defended his opinion about dialectical materialism and Brechtian theatre with casual ease, completely ignorant of the strings his words were teasing, I think he did not even notice me that day—not really—but he had my complete attention. It was not long before I became a regular at his luncheon discourses. Often, I would find fault with his personal treatment of the subjects and he would pull me into learned arguments about principles and moral liberty. Our conversations were so engaging that we would call each other to discuss portions we recently read in a magazine or a book. After a time, the conversations started taking new routes and we found ourselves discussing each other as much as our academic standpoints. We would meet for lunches on holidays and spend Saturdays in galleries and cafes. I fell in love with Amrit and him with me, but I cannot say when. We dated for over a year and had a long sexual tryst before we married, and it seemed like the happiest time of my life.

Marriage was not the uptight, bare fare they make it to be. For both of us, life was much the same—the same jobs, the same social circles, the same impassioned conversations, the same intimacy and the same easy understanding of each other. Of course there were new facets to our relationship and new responsibilities, but the essence of the union remained true. Our families were as happy for us as we were and the times were kind to us.

In the third year of our marriage, we came to know that we could not have children. For my mother, it was shattering news. But we dealt with it. We even considered adopting a child, but neither of us found the courage to raise another's child as our own. With time, we came to be at peace with it and life regained a semblance of normalcy. I took a break from teaching. We shifted into a house of our own. Amrit was always strong and supportive of me. Lost in his dialogues or in his arms, I soon put the sorrow behind me too.

All things changed when Ritesh showed up at my door one morning. Amrit was in one of his lectures and I had been home when the doorbell rang. I unlatched the door and there he was. Taller, broader of frame and face and with his hairline just beginning to fall back from his forehead, but his eyes were the same, and his smile, when it came, pushed through my initial confusion and made me gasp. But what he did next was even more unbelievable. He stepped up, swept me into his arms, and before I could react, kissed me full on my lips.

He knew I was married. He must have known it very well. He must have seen the vermillion on my forehead, the locket around my neck. He should have stayed away, or said his greetings and gone. But he kissed me, the fool. And think what you may of me, without my fully realizing what was happening, I kissed him back. It was much like the kisses from my teenage romance, only this time we were both adults and his touch tantalized me as no one's touch ever had. There were no introductions, no bitter words, no joyous reconciliation. There just was that tide of passion he threw against my walls, and soon my senses were flooded with him. I think we made you on that first day, the first time we lay together. Amrit never knew and he never suspected, even when I missed my period. When I could not hide it anymore and he came to know, he presumed that he was going to be a father despite all that the doctors had said. Much as it pained me, I had accepted the loss of my marriage much before it really came to it. Some part of my subconscious must have known it since the day I saw him in my doorway, that first day. We had struck a fire that day which I knew I could not stop. It was going to burn down my home and I knew I did not have the courage to douse it.

Ritesh became a constant secret in my life. I gave birth to you and named you Vivant because that was the name Amrit wanted you to have. Then, a month later, I left both him and you without a word of parting or an apology. I left with Ritesh and we moved to Mumbai. It was a whirlwind romance and it was good till the very end. In 1998, he died of flu and left me alone and childless. And so I have been, since then to this day, and that is how I am going to go. The doctors say I have cancer and I do not have many days left.

Most days the pain is such that I cannot hold a pen straight or get myself to sit. But I am writing this to you today, while I have the time, not to explain why I left or to apologize for wrongs already done. No, son. I have missed you all my life and will die missing you. I could not know you in life, nor you, me, and a letter can only talk one way, so I am giving you a window to see me through. What you make of me is a choice you have to make.

Love,
Your mother, Ishani

The Ice Cream Man

ARKA BASU

Kunal Singh had patrolled these streets for nearly thirty years, and this had earned him the reputation of being the neighbourhood's 'most wary cop'. He often regarded this title with pride and boasted no other ice cream man would ever hold such a post.

But times had changed rapidly since he was a young boy with a new ice cream cart selling old favourites like tutti fruity and kesar pista. As more people began to call the city their own, there opened many ice cream parlours to cater to their wants and over time, deaf ears were turned to his regular chants of vanilla, chocolate and butterscotch ice cream. These parlours had bright, plush, air conditioned interiors with seating arrangements for many customers. Their variety of ice creams far exceeded what his little cart could hold, and the guarantees of selling low-fat ice creams was one he could not adhere to. Thus, over time his sales plunged and he had to look for work elsewhere.

He still patrolled the streets with his white ice cream cart, which had the words 'Icy Dreams' painted across, but his profession had vastly changed. His voice never grew weary these days, and the once raspy tone of his cry played out in his mind like an old song. He was the very symbol of silence as he walked down the streets pushing his cart along the boulevards of the suburbs.

Little children, who were still innocent to the enchantments of advertisements and commercialization often ran to his cart longing for some old favourites from times long past. He had to turn them away saying he had unfortunately finished his day's stock. Their disappointment was hard to bear, and a long face was particularly agonizing to a man who had been making kids smile for so many years, but what choice did he have? Life had to be worked for.

His little green mobile phone began to vibrate in his pocket and he clicked the answer button to hear a familiar voice.

'Kunal, there's a garden party on Leslie Street around 5 o' clock this evening, I need you to supply the desserts,' spoke the man on the line.

Kunal smiled.

Business.

The city had grown around him through his days; every year new skyscrapers would rise, conquering a little more of the visible sky. The roads were no more filled with the trills of bicycle bells and the occasional vehicle. On the contrary, bicycles were rarely seen, while vehicles seemed to breed at the same alarming rate as the city's residents. Development was continual; every day there were roads being paved, underpasses being dug and bridges being constructed. Yet, it seemed to Kunal that the more convenience people tried to bring into their lives, the more adverse grew their complications.

Beggars stood near the sidewalk, patiently waiting for the traffic light to turn red so they could collect enough coins to pay their handlers for a scanty meal. This was a common sight despite the government deciding to bring in several remedies to help the poor and the destitute who roamed the street in search of work or alms. Kunal knew the ancient philosophy—for the rich to be rich, the poor would have to remain poor. The officials working for the state weren't getting any poorer so he knew what fate awaited the needy.

Living on the streets was known to him, and the first fifteen years of his life as a roadside vagrant had taught him more valuable lessons than all his other years put together. As a child, Kunal had learned that money was a force to be reckoned with. It placed people in their individual stations and gave some men sports cars to drive in and others fruit carts to drag along throughout their brief lives. He knew money tended to perpetually attract every form of mortal danger; the wealth-induced crimes that he had witnessed as a child had never completely worn off from his mind. Indeed, money probably stole a person's peace of mind, but it did quench the constant voracity that ate at his innards night and day. Money was, in all honesty, life.

Kunal had certainly risen above the station of a street dweller, although it seemed to him that it was all just a cruel lending of fate. Just when he thought life was being a little kind, just when ice cream had become the sole evening sensation, just when he began to pride himself upon the fact that he too was a valuable asset of this society, time decided he had had his share.

Like all living entities, this city had a beating heart, but technology and expansion had drawn all of its efforts over the years. Now everyone lived secluded lives in their little grotto-like apartments, too busy to come out and spend a little time in the company of others. No one longed for a cone of ice cream under the searing sun anymore; people bought in bulk what the supermarkets housed for the masses. The joys of walking through a crowded park on a hot summer day, being fully aware that ice cream would bring about the greatest delight—that was the feeling he missed the most. No crowds ever haunted the parks anymore; they lay as desolate reminders of how things were at a better time.

He had not forgotten his roots; he often stopped at street corners to distribute a few ice lollies to little children who performed petty tricks to earn a meagre sum to support their families. He was luckier than them, and in acknowledgement he gave away a little of what he earned. Yet, there were always so many mouths to feed, and so few who cared. He did what he could, as would befit an ice cream man.

By the corner of Fajwal Road, there stood a little tea shop which seemed to have been unaffected by the tides of time. The green tin exteriors had been faded as long as Kunal could remember, yet the old HMT clock still stood on the opposite wall showing how many hours were left of each day. There was also a little black radio which interrupted everyone by constantly mumbling reports of happenings around the country. The old shopkeeper, Gurbaj, who had been serving tea for almost six decades saw Kunal and genially smiled. He had been one of the few customers who had remained faithful to the tea he had served for so many years, and what was more, he always stopped to talk.

'Kunal Singh! It's good to see you! Masala tea?' Gurbaj asked as he walked to the back of his shop to bring out two glasses from the little cupboard.

'Yes sir. How are you doing? I haven't passed by this way for over a week now. I'm hoping everything is alright?' Kunal replied as he searched around the shop for the daily newspaper.

'Yes, yes, everything is fine as usual. My niece is getting married this week, so I have been very busy of late. People only get married once, so I must do my bit,' the old man said as he stirred the vessel of heated milk.

'Indeed sir. To live is to serve,' Kunal replied as he finally fished out the local newspaper from beneath an earthen pot.

'Here you are,' spoke the shopkeeper, putting down two glasses of tea and picking one up to sip the hot concoction while it was still warm.

Kunal sipped the delicious masala tea and read the headlines of the day. Varun Malik, a silverware business man, living uptown, had been murdered in cold blood in the late hours of the night. Crime had only one true purpose: to keep growing.

'Pradhan came along this morning; he wanted me to give you this. Something he brought back from Vaishno Devi, after his son recovered from malaria. God watches over his children, does he not?' Gurbaj questioned as he finished the last dregs of his tea.

'Indeed he does. I'm relieved Pradhan's son is alright now; things weren't looking too good for him. Thank him for me, will you?' The ice cream man told the old shopkeeper, as he put his cup down and licked his lips.

'Of course. You have a good day, and drop by anytime,' Gurbaj said as Kunal collected the package, waved and began to wheel his ice cream cart away.

He entered the city park and sat down on a solitary bench. He was getting too old for his job, and he wondered how much longer his limbs would support him. Kunal closed his eyes for a few moments and listened to the music of the springtime birds. The leaves of the few trees that remained, rustled with the passing breeze and he nearly felt that emotion that envelopes every other feeling in an ocean of serenity. Yet, in a moment the distant sounds of the city came rushing back to his ears and it was lost once again.

The sky began to show the first traces of amber as the sun dipped down to embrace the evening. He saw birds returning from their daily jaunts to rest under the blanket of the approaching night. Kunal got up and began to push his ice cream cart along the road out of the park into the elegant avenue.

In about fifteen minutes, he reached the end of the road and waited outside the last bungalow on the right. It had a well-organized garden, and the thriving lilies caught his attention; he had always liked those flowers. As he waited, he whistled to himself, a practice every waiter in the world would have tried to adopt at some point of their lives.

A man in a tweed suit exited the house and walked to the garage. He was young, clearly not very worn by this world and his demeanour showed an opulent upbringing. The streets were empty now, but soon the humdrum of chaos would begin once the offices closed around the city. Kunal fished around his pockets to find Pradhan's package. He opened the seal and turned it over in his hand; a silencer landed on his palm. *Perfect.*

'Mr Leslie?' Kunal cried as he looked for a certain article inside the folds of his jacket. The man nodded, and began to walk his way.

Out of his breast pocket Kunal took out his treasured Glock G21 revolver and shot the man thrice across the chest. Quickly, he wheeled his cart into position and began to place the corpse into the freezing chamber. The Director would love this, for was there ever a better proof of a finished job than a dead body?

In a few minutes, it was all over and Kunal wheeled his cart down the darkening boulevard. He missed his former job.

ॐ

The Book Signing

ARKA BASU

She stood by the entrance of The Leather Company, and wondered why there were so many reporters at Madison Mall on a Tuesday. Weekdays were the precious few hours that compulsive shoppers had, to fulfil their weekly shopping needs. Yet, with such an abundance of press coverage inside the mall, no shopper could feel the surge of spending nirvana that one was usually allowed on such a day.

'What is happening here today? Why are there so many reporters around?' she asked a fellow shopper who was comparing a set of burgundy handbags inside the well-lit store.

'Don't you know? Johir Pratap is here today! He will be delivering a speech to aspiring young writers at Landmark, following which he will sign copies of his newest book,' the woman answered as she finally decided on one of the two handbags.

Johir Pratap was a well-known novelist who had been writing for a little over half a decade, and his books were not unknown to her. He was not the stereotypical writer who lived a secluded life behind his pages, but a rather active author who travelled a fair deal around the country promoting his books, giving speeches to inspire new writers and working with the public to raise awareness on principal issues. His reputation of being a fine orator had been noticed by publishers too, and many youth-oriented magazines quoted him in various articles. Yet, she remembered Johir Pratap as someone else.

She decided her shopping could wait a few hours; she would not shop in such commotion even if the stores decided to start clearance sales a month before. Also, the writer's speech held a rarer charm for her and indeed, how often did one get to meet with an old friend?

Landmark was usually packed with avid readers, but on that particular day the crowd comprised more than just people who appreciated great books. There were middle-aged executives who usually stopped by for an early lunch, little boys who spent all their lives in the arcade downstairs, delusional duchesses who sparkled with exaggerated fashion statements and solitary men with little notepads, who were certainly unpublished writers trying to obtain a handful of pointers.

Up ahead, in front of the bustling TV crew, who ferreted around the little clearing as if to practice the art of stepping over camera wires, stood Johir Pratap, the man of the day. Her memories of him still painted a nearly accurate picture of his countenance, albeit the years had made him lose a fair share of his once shaggy hair. A pair of spectacles balanced on his bony nose like a stalwart, as if to defend those soft, deep-set eyes. His face had matured, although it seemed that days, not years had permanently left their mark on him. Such was a writer's life, she thought to herself.

'Now I know you all are here for one or two or three reasons: Because you love writing and you believe my advice can help you write better; because you want a signed copy of my new book or because you want to be on TV. If the second or third reason pertains to you, please stay, but if you love writing, what are you doing here? Get to it!'

'I'm joking, please remain by all means, although my advice to you can only do so much as a lighter does to a stove, I can merely give you that spark. But it is up to you to keep the fire burning, to keep your story alive despite the rough winds of disbelief and discomfort, through every pitfall and peak, until you reach the final page of your novel. Yet, you must endure still, until you reach the very last line, the very last word and the very last letter. And only then will you be a writer.'

'Life will not be nice to you; niceties are for other people with stable jobs and fixed pay cheques. Your life will be filled with every drawback that nature can contrive, to stall and shake you off the path of your choosing. Horrible coffee, frequent heartaches, a lack of belief in your abilities, being fired from your day job are all a part of the package you have signed up for. So, when misfortune arrives at your doorstep, provided you still have a roof over your head, remember he's not leaving anytime soon. Entertain him with your tale, tell him your story, maybe even lend him your pen for a few days, but make sure you keep him busy, and keep writing…'

She was awed by how fame had instilled a sense of confidence in his character, something that she had never seen in his younger days. Although the crowd was frolicking around before, most people now stood quite engrossed in the writer's speech, which seemed to have the same spellbinding effect as his novels. Notepads were being etched in furiously as enthusiastic fingers produced an eerie symphony of pen on paper, and writers were being born inside minds that had always longed to write.

'I better conclude this speech before I bore you all to the grave, following which you will never buy another novel of mine.

Remember, writing is not merely a passion, it's a profession, so take it as a day job, be your own boss, evaluate each product like you'd pay anything to possess it, live in the world of your words as much as you live in this other realm, and for God's sake, keep writing!'

She had seen earnest applause, but never him at the receiving end of it; things had clearly changed from her school days. The once shy boy who was regularly tormented by stage fright when made to read in class, now looked on with all smiles at everyone present in the bookstore. She applauded too just as she had done years and years ago.

Her mind could recall only flashes of distinct memories from the days of her adolescence, but some of these memories had stuck in her mind as bookmarks to events that one often flips back to when life's present chapter seems to lose its charm. They had been in the same class for nearly two years before she had to leave school because her father had gotten transferred. Being new to a school was never a pleasant prospect, even less so when one had grown up, and yet she had made friends rather easily in that modest span of time. Being the only other person in an elective French class, she had met Johir, whose only interest in the subject was reading the original works of Henri Bosco and Guy de Maupassant.

While he did not talk much initially, she thought he was one of those introverts who lived only for the joys of scholastic grades. It took her a little over a month to realize that he was in fact too lost in thought for most of his days to spare time for empty conversation. But boredom took over him eventually, and soon he began to exhibit his more garrulous side. Johir was not of the regular twine; his mind had been sewn with a different thread, and for this reason he did not spend too much time in the company of many people at school. He feared the stage with the same dread as most children fear darkness and wild beasts. The trepidation was more than evident on his face every time he was forced to deliver a speech, which happened to be a yearly requisite for every student. Unlike most boys and girls who longed to pursue careers in law or medicine, Johir had always wanted to be a writer, fully aware that such a profession could never be counted as a full-fledged job. He enjoyed writing short stories in particular, claiming that they held the essence of many novels, in but a few pages. As he did not have too many friends to discuss his work with, she soon became his esteemed critic.

Johir was a likeable chap, with more knowledge than one could foresee upon first sight, and time flew in his company, as time often does in a story. Yet, that was precisely the problem.

Before the end of the final term, she first caught wind of her father's impending transfer. When she conveyed the same to Johir, a part of him seemed to be overthrown, a part of him that had always feared the limelight and solitude, which most noticed but seldom cared. He tried to reason with her and she with him, as immaturity always swears by undying hope, even where there is none. But for all their plans to find her a temporary place to stay to finish her schooling it amounted to nothing. On their last day, Johir wrote her a short story, and though she could not recall what it was about, she remembered savouring it dearly. In the end when she left, stoic as he was, he lost more than an amateur critic, though she wondered if he still remembered her.

He did not write to her, nor had he replied to the initial letters that she had sent him from her new home, and she expected distance had done their friendship no favours. Maybe, he had found a new critic, though that seemed to be an unlikely event.

Many years passed, and new friends gently erased memories of old friendships, and Johir became another faded picture in the depths of her mind, until one day when she saw his face again.

Every month, *The Sentry Writer* published an article about a new, upcoming writer, and from a tiny frame in the cover, Johir stared back at her. She celebrated in silence as she read the article in which he had outlined his journey from a yearning writer of short stories to a published author, with all the trials along the way. She smiled as she remembered she had been his first critic.

His fame grew over time, as often happens with writers who have a knack for producing bestsellers, and she heard his name far more often as the days passed. She wanted to get back in touch with him, but hesitated, not knowing how fame might have changed him over the years. Not wanting to resemble a moth which longs for the flame of fame, she let it pass.

Surely procrastination could no more be a solution to abstain from yet another attempt at getting back in touch, but she felt too unnerved to approach the famous writer in the midst of so many people. Instead she decided to join the line that was forming for the book signing event to commence. With a copy of the newly released *Remembering the Dream* tucked under her arm she waited behind an array of people who seemed to be in a frenzy to meet the author of the book.

She knew not what to expect at the other end, but it cheered her immensely to realize that she had left her inhibition in the past and the future bore only fond memories of days gone by. Friends once, friends forever—that was what she lived by, and most of her childhood friends kept in touch with her. Even if he didn't remember her, she still remembered him, and her features hadn't altered as his, so his recollection would probably be brought back to life upon laying eyes on her again.

But what if he didn't? There was always a possibility that so much had transpired in his life that that any shadowy memory about her might have been washed away by later events, which had surely held more bearing in his mind. What then? Would she walk away from his desk just as another fan of his books would, upon getting his or her copy signed? The queue had now shortened, and she could not bring herself to quit the line.

Finally, after a gentleman in a pinstriped jacket shook Johir's hand and departed with his novel, she came face to face with the acclaimed writer.

'Hello!' he said with the same infallible smile as he reached for his fountain pen to autograph her novel.

'Hi! Johir—' she stuttered, and yet could not bring herself to ask him whether he remembered her or not. The sound of his name seemed to have made his astute eyes flicker for a moment, but that was all.

'Don't worry, I'll return your book after I've signed my name on it; you have the bill to prove that it's truly yours,' he chuckled as he noticed she still had the novel carefully tucked under her arm. A few people laughed at hearing this, and she blushed as she placed the novel on his desk. He did not ask for a name to sign it off to, or for that matter, not even as a hint of courtesy. He just looked back at her with the same undying smile until she realized it was time to move away.

She returned home and lay down on her bed, pleading with herself to see reason. How could he have remembered? It hadn't been a few years, it had been more than a decade, and it seemed pure folly to expect him to remember her at sudden sight. Yet, hope, that tiny flame that lends light to dwellers in the darkest dungeons, had shown her a different outcome to this meeting. Even so, hope had failed her, and she closed her eyes wishing the day had never occurred.

She could not fall asleep as her catalogue of ancient memories burst forth like a thunder cloud showering her inner eyes with forgotten memories. Had he truly forgotten about their friendship? Or was this his way of intimating indifference to her leaving? Perhaps that had left a permanent mark on his nature, and he had decided that the mind does life no favours by remembering lost thoughts long after their footprints have faded, as she was coming to accept now.

She needed a distraction, and she noticed the new novel lying on her bedside table beside her. She had forgotten about it in the midst of a million melancholic thoughts. Quietly she opened the book, unsure of whether it would be of any help to her in her present state of emotional dilemma.

Unable to find the author's autograph on the first page, she flipped to the second, where she read, in printed, clear cut characters: her name.

He had remembered.

Contributors

Lipi Mehta (Editor)

Lipi Mehta struggles less with reading than she does with writing though she can seldom pick just one between the two.

Adithya Narayanan

Adithya Narayanan is a Teach for India Fellow, teaching a 5th grade class of sixty-one kids in Malwani—Asia's second largest slum. When he's not teaching his kids, he's either playing football, writing or looking out of the window of a bus, planning his own revolution.

Anant Tripathi

Anant Tripathi had the good fortune of growing up ignorant of the possibilities of the written word. Today, not many years thence, he struggles anew each day to write his novel and prepares for the day his first manuscript will receive its first rejection—when the ad production business gives him a minute, that is.

Neha Joshi

Neha Joshi is a journalist by degree and a teacher by choice. She spends her time eating, cooking and dreaming about good food when she isn't teaching a class of seven-year-olds to dream big.

Hina Siddiqui

Hina Siddiqui writes and creates drama on a daily basis. Literally. Her last play *White Noise* was notoriously acclaimed, almost to the point of being stopped on stage by the moral police. Her special skills include challenging the patriarchy, questioning traditional belief systems and making one heck of an omelette. She can be reached at hinaqui@gmail.com

Aniroodha Mukherjee

Born in Ajmer, Aniroodha is a photographer, writer and public health management enthusiast. For his stories, he draws inspiration from his upbringing and loves writing about the small things in life. He is currently pursuing his master's in public health from Delhi.

Srinidhi Raghavan

Srinidhi currently lives in a space between reality and an alternate universe with pixies, fairies and female superheroes. Her everyday work involves working on issues regarding women and child rights. She writes to make sense of this complicated world.

Aniket Dasgupa

Aniket Dasgupta is a film-maker, writer, graphic designer and Earl Grey activist among many other things. He loves travelling and hates stagnancy. When not pursuing existential quests, he questions why the universe does what it does.

Tnahsin Garg

Tnahsin is a young, restless wanderer who is currently exploring Europe while pursuing his Ph.D. His first novel *The Prophecy of Trivine* of the science fiction genre will be soon released. The curious ones can find him at http://tnahsingarg.tumblr.com/.

T. Nandagopal

T. Nandagopal is a working engineer. He is interested in writing about things and people with subtler shades of meaning than is normally attributed to them. He considers himself influenced heavily by Oscar Wilde, James Joyce and to a lesser extent, Jhumpa Lahiri. Other than writing, his interests include football and music.

Arka Basu

Arka Basu is a student of English Literature. He has an avid interest in experimental and traditional forms of poetry. He wishes to continue writing short stories which explore the nature of companionship, the immutability of social barriers and the philosophy of art.

Janice Rodrigues

Janice Rodrigues is a journalism graduate of Wilson College, Mumbai. In her spare time she enjoys meeting people, having new experiences, going on endless sitcom sprees and just appreciating life. Sometimes she even manages to do a little writing! You can contact her at janice_remita@hotmail.com.

Mona Ramavat

Mona Ramavat is a writer and journalist based in Hyderabad. She has written for various publications over a career spanning a decade and is currently with *India Today*. Besides cutting-edge lifestyle reporting, she indulges her creativity with poetry, short stories and scribbles.

Kiren Jogi

For Kiren Jogi, writing is an added feather to her cap of many talents. She is a renowned actor from Birmingham who has had a successful career in the UK after graduating from the University of Aberystwyth in Drama, Performance and Film Studies. She features in advertisements and Bollywood films as well.

Sneh Thakur

Sneh Thakur is a brand and innovation junkie who has worked with leading FMCG brands. Born in Kuwait, she travelled her way from refugee camps during the Kuwait war to study in Dehradun, Delhi, Indore and Pune. She currently lives in Dubai and describes herself best in five words, 'Pint-sized Rapunzel. On a cloud'.

Naman Saraiya

Naman Saraiya is a writer, journalist and a photographer based in Mumbai.

Kailash Srinivasan

Kailash Srinivasan published his first book, *What Happened to That Love*, a short story collection, in 2010, and is currently working on his second book. Apart from this, some of his work has appeared in *Urban Shots – Love Collection*, *Chicken Soup* series of books, and in literary magazines in India and Australia.

Esha Vaish

Esha Vaish is a financial journalist with Thomson Reuters. Having previously contributed an article in the *Expressive Self* creative writing course book, the author has always had a keen interest in fiction writing. She has a bachelor's degree in journalism from Symbiosis Institute of Media and Communication (UG).

Aakash Karkare

Aakash is a movie buff and loves movies from all over the world. He studies media at Sophia Polytechnic and is twenty-one year old. He loves playing tennis and even reads and writes about it. Do check out his web series, *Incredible Indians*, where he showcases his short films and videos.

Tejal Johri

Tejal Johri is twenty-two years old and is currently pursuing her Master's degree in Economics from the Energy and Resource Institute, New Delhi. She is a fan of J. M. Coetzee's writing and loves reading and writing. She travels in her spare time and is obsessed with good indie rock music.

Arpita Bohra

Arpita Bohra is a Literature Graduate who is wrapping up her Masters in Counselling. She feels writing and psychotherapy involve the same process—an intense and sensitive engagement with stories and narratives; the imagined, the lived and the possible. Read more of her writings at http://angelwitchdiaries.blogspot.in

Naomi Sarah

Naomi Sarah is an online writer with her very own website in the pipeline. When she's not reading, she dreams of waking up in Paris.